CW00404912

Three Words

Ashlee Rose

Ashlee Rose
Copyright © 2023 Ashlee Rose

First Edition

Model: Mason Castello
Photographer: Stacy Powell (SP Cover Photography)

The author has asserted their moral right under the Copyright, Designs and
Patents Act, 1988, to be identified as the author of this work.

All rights reserved. No part of this publication may be reproduced, copied,
stored in a retrieval system, or transmitted, in any form by or by any means,
without the prior written consent of the copyright holder, nor be otherwise
circulated in any form of binding or cover other than that in which it is
published and without a similar condition being imposed on the subsequent
purchaser.

This is a work of fiction. Names, characters, businesses, places, events and
incidents are either the products of the authors imagination or used in a
fictitious manner.
Any resemblance to actual persons, living or dead, or actual events is purely
coincidental.

For all the readers wanting a 'big boy' to call them a 'good girl'

Other Books By Ashlee Rose

Entwined in You Series:

Something New

Something To Lose

Something Everlasting

Before Her

Without Her

Forever Her

Standalones:

Unwanted

Promise Me

Savage Love

Tortured Hero

Something Worth Stealing

Dear Heart, You Screwed Me

Signed, Sealed, Baby

Duet:

Love Always, Peyton

Forever Always, Knight

Way Back When Duet

Novellas:

Welcome to Rosemont

Rekindle Us

Your Dirty Little Secret

Seeking Hallow

A Savage Reunion

Risqué Reads:

Seeking Hallow

Craving Hex

Seducing Willow

All available on Amazon Kindle Unlimited

Only suitable for 18+ due to nature of the books.

Prologue

THIRTY-THREE.

I am thirty-three.

Sitting here surrounded by my friends and family as they sing happy birthday to me. I love birthdays, or I used to love birthdays when I was a kid and excited about getting the latest barbie doll. But now the realisation hits me like a freight train.

I was alone. I wasn't getting any younger and I had the worst dating history so settling down was not going to happen anytime soon.

'Happy birthday to Cody...'

I jolt from my thoughts, plastering on a fake smile as I blow out the candles on my numbered cake, just reminding me of my age.

I felt like I was failing at life.

No man.

No ring.

No kids.

No three words telling me just how much I mean to someone.

It's just three little words; three words that can change your life. They shouldn't mean as much as they do, but they do. Those three powerful words. But does anyone really mean it when they say it? How easy is it just to let them slip off your tongue? *I love you.*

It's as easy as a lie.

Three little words that hold the power over your life and choices.

Three little words that can ruin you in an instant, yet we still crave hearing them. Feeling them.

I used to want to hear them, but that was then... and well, well this is now.

Chapter One

18th Birthday

"COME ON CODY, WE NEED TO GET READY!" MY FRIEND Hallie called, banging on the door as I brushed my teeth. I tapped my phone screen with my knuckle to look at the time. Shoot.

"Coming!" I shouted out, spitting and rinsing my mouth as I tightened my towel around my slender body and run for the bedroom.

I saw Hallie, Mable and Tia all standing looking at me, arms crossed against their chest.

"We're going to be late, I booked us VIP with George, he pulled a lot of strings to get us in, don't blow this Cody!" Mable scowled at me. I held my hand up indicating I was sorry as I rushed to my walk-in closet, grabbing a little black dress and killer heels. I dropped the towel, shimmying into my seamless thong and bra.

"You think this dress, yes?" I asked as I held the tiny scrap of material that had one shoulder covered in a floral detail.

They all nodded.

"You'll look hot, and we need to find you someone to go home with," Hallie smiled as she looked at my other two friends.

I rolled my eyes, shaking my head from side to side. I pulled my dress up my legs and over my hips then slipping one arm through the dress. It was a stretchy material so I could pull it lower or higher.

My brown hair was already down and straight, sitting just under my breasts.

I grabbed my bag and spritzed myself with my perfume then slipped my feet into the black, strapped sandals.

"Ready?" I asked.

"Ready!" The girls sung as we clinked our canned cocktails and knocked them back. Nothing like a bit of Dutch courage.

This was our weekends. Every weekend. My birthday was the seventeenth, but whatever day it fell on, we had a girl's night whether that be in, and if it was the weekend we were definitely out.

Giggling as we walked cautiously down the stairs, I really didn't want to break my ankle on my birthday.

As we got to the bottom of the stairs, my father stood in front of the door, crossing his arms across his chest.

He coughed, clearing his throat as his eyes glided up and down my body.

"Young lady..." he trailed off.

I rolled my eyes, causing a snigger off the girls.

"And you three, either pull the dresses down where they should be or go back upstairs and get changed."

My dad was a tall man, his eyes a honey colour, his hair thick black and pushed back from his face.

"Tony," my mum called out, swatting him with a tea towel. "Leave them alone. Girls you look beautiful. Go and have fun, don't be too late and text me once you get to the club and when you're leaving. Do you have your key?" She asked me. She seemed so small and tiny compared to my dad. She had dark blonde hair, a heart shaped face and green eyes which popped against her pale complexion. My dad looked down at her, pulling her close to him and smiling.

My heart swelled at the love they had for each other. They had been together since college. My dad a lawyer, my mum a legal secretary. In the end, my dad set up a law firm and they worked side by side until my dad retired and sold his business.

He offered it to me, but I declined. As much as I would have loved to work there, I was more creative, a free spirit and I didn't want to be chained down to a desk from nine to five.

"Thanks mum," I smiled, looking back at the girls before waving at my parents and hopping into the waiting taxi.

PULLING KERBSIDE AT THE CLUB, THE MUSIC WAS booming. George was standing on the door, his eyes glistening as they locked on Mable. She blushed a beautiful crimson as she got closer to him. George unclipped the red rope and let us through.

"Happy Birthday Cody," he smiled.

"Thank you." I smiled back as we walked in to check our coats in. Stepping into the club, 'Closer' – Ne-Yo was pumping through the speakers.

"Let's dance!" I shouted as I led them to the dance floor, wiggling my hips as I did.

· · ·

I WOKE THE NEXT MORNING, MY HEAD HURT BUT I FELT okay. Rolling onto my side I noticed the thick, blonde-haired boy still sleeping on his front next to me.

I smiled. I sat up, pulling the bedsheet round my chest as I waited for him to wake. Pinching my cheeks to put a little colour into them and running my fingers through my hair I let my eyes roam up and down his back. His muscles rippled under his back as he moved, turning and looking at me.

"Morning," I blushed.

"Hey," he smiled before pushing himself up and looking around the room. He twisted, sitting up and resting against the headboard.

"Last night was..." I nibbled my bottom lip. His hand wrapped around the back of his head as he rubbed it.

"Yeah..." he sighed before his blue eyes found mine. "I need you to go... you know... before my parents wake."

I felt my heart twist, my stomach knot.

"Oh, yeah, of course." I half laugh as I slip out of the bed, taking the sheet with me. I pick my discarded clothes off the floor and slip them on as gracefully as I can without revealing all of myself again.

Picking up my phone from the bedside table, it was only six forty-five.

"You wanna exchange numbers? Maybe we can go for a drink or something?" He asked which caused a smile to slip onto my lips.

"Sure, I would like that," I nodded as I took his phone, typing my number in.

"Cool," he winked.

"Cool," I repeated his words as I walked for the bedroom door. He was hot on my heels, wrapping his arm around my waist and placing a kiss on my cheek. "Happy birthday Cody."

Three Words

I never did hear from him.
But it was okay, there were plenty more fish in the sea.

Chapter Two

Present Day

"READY FOR DINNER TONIGHT?" MABEL ASKS AS SHE twists her wedding band and engagement ring round on her finger.

"Yup," I smiled, arranging the bouquet I was working on.

"Good, I need a drink. Rocco has been a nightmare, teething and wanting to constantly feed on me. I need a good pump and dump tonight." She sighed, her elbows resting on the counter as I worked.

"That bad?" I asked.

She rolled her eyes, "Yes, that bad. I am exhausted." She said through a yawn which made me yawn. "I like that bouquet, reminds me of my wedding bouquet that you had done for our wedding." She says, smiling fondly. "I love George, but my god. I am so envious of him sometimes, he goes to the clubs, scouts and mingles with the big names while I am at home being a constant feeding machine." She groans as she spins her now empty coffee cup.

"I know, I can imagine it's hard." I sighed, throwing out the same answers I normally do when she has her moments like this. I don't mean to, but I go into auto pilot.

"That's why I can't wait for tonight. George can stay home with Rocco, and I can go out, eat and drink in peace without a crying baby attached to my bullet nipples."

I scoff, tipping my head back and laughing.

"Bullet nipples." I shake my head.

"You laugh Cody, this'll be you soon, you enjoy the full night's sleep you're getting and enjoy your full, perky tits because as soon as you have a baby, they literally suck the life out of them, and you're left with empty, saggy sandbags. I have told George for my thirty-fifth birthday I want new boobs," she huffs.

"Oo new boobs? So that means no more babies?" I ask as I admire my work, smiling.

"Definitely no more babies. My vagina is battered and if I am having new boobs, I am not having another baby to ruin them." She winces at her words. "That sounds harsh," she says quietly and rubs her lips into a thin line.

"Not at all, it's your life and your body. If you're okay with just having the one, then you do you." I lean over the counter and rub the top of her arm.

"I just feel awful because Hallie is having a hard time trying to conceive her first and has started IVF."

"You can't feel awful, there is nothing you can do hun. Hallie will fall, I know it," I chime as I place the flowers into the cooler out back, Mabel following behind me.

"And then there is Tia, on her third husband and pregnant with her first. I feel like I have no one to really vent to apart from you because well..." She stopped.

I smirk, turning to face her.

"Because I am single, alone and will never have a child

because I can't hold down a steady relationship? Oh wait, I can't even get to the relationship stage because I either get ghosted or humped and dumped and by the next morning I'm left in my bed, alone. No point going back to their places anymore, it's a lot better if I let the hoppys stay at mine."

"Hoppys?" Mable cocks her head to the side, her perfectly shaped brows furrow and pull.

"Yeah, I've given up remembering their names. Hoppy suits. It's easy to remember and they are just that. They come home to mine, we fuck like rabbits and then they hop out of my nice warm bed and back to whatever vermin hole they came from."

She doesn't say anything.

"So yeah, vent away," I wink as I walk back out front and open my order book. Mabel follows me, running her palms down her skirt as she swallows.

"Busy?" She asks, quickly changing the subject.

"Yup, not long till wedding season." My tone was clipped, but not because of Mabel, but because of my reality. It comes on suddenly, and when it does it hits me like a tsunami.

"I'm sorry Cody." Mabel's voice was quiet, her perfectly manicured nails scratching on her skin as she fidgets, restlessness apparent.

"Oh, please don't be sorry," I look up at her and smile, "it's just a kick in the teeth when I think about all the fuck ups throughout the years."

"You'll find him soon." She tries to reassure me.

"Mm, and pigs fly," I shrug up, closing my order book shut and checking my emails.

"Cody..."

"Look, I'm not going to hold my breath, because if I do,

10

I'll die. I am fine with my life; I own my own home, I have a beautiful florist company I run with my mum, and I have the three best friends anyone could wish for, honestly... I am fine with my life." I lied. Because that's how easy it is now, the small white lies I tell myself and other people are comforting to me.

Mabel looks at her watch. "Babe, I've got to go, I have to get Rocco home before he wakes," she turns to look at her doting son sleeping in his pram.

"No worries, I'll see you in a bit," I smile at her as I look to where her gaze is glued to the beautiful red headed sleeping boy.

"See you at seven," she kisses me on the cheek before walking out of the shop.

And I was alone again.

But it's fine.

It's always fine.

I am always fine.

I finished work early, locking up and heading to the gym. I needed to burn off some pent-up tension and energy and a workout would do just that. After an hour had passed, I patted my wet face off with a towel and headed for home. Smiling as I approached my front door, I let myself into my home and sighed with relief when I shut the door. The silence welcomed me, and suddenly, the loneliness crashed over me. I try to imagine my life with a doting husband, little brown-haired twins running round the hallways as they scream with laughter and hearing the cute I love yous and me being the perfect mum that makes them feel nothing but love.

I was pulled from my daydream when my phone

pinged. I knew that sound. That sound used to fill me with excitement where now it just feels me with disappointment.

Fisting in my bag I pull my phone out to see a notification from one of my many dating apps. I was tempted to click and open it but decided against it. I needed to shower and get ready for tonight; I didn't want to be late for my own birthday dinner and drinks.

I walked through my hallway, the natural light coming through from the floor to ceiling window that was at the end of the hallway and overlooking the city skyline. I decorated the rooms in beiges, creams, golds and taupes. I wanted all the rooms neutral and the furniture the same so I could accessorise with any colours and not have to change the décor as such. I had high ceilings, thick coving hugging them and beautiful, vintage ceiling roses. The house I lived in was an old Victorian town house. Some were converted to flats, and some were kept as just that, town houses. I loved the character and the beauty that fills it. When me and my mum took the loan out to buy the florist, I always said I wanted it to be successful enough for me to buy my forever home and that's exactly what I did.

We bought the shop off a lovely couple called Taron and Luna. It wasn't just a florist; it was also a cake and coffee shop. It was perfect. I added a little book corner into a large open space that I felt needed a little more and I can't even begin to tell you how nice it is to see the amount of people who sit all cosy in the bat winged chairs and read.

I sigh as I slip my clothes off and hop into the shower. I clip my hair up, so I don't get it wet; it's already styled in loose waves from this morning. I feel my tense muscles begin to relax as I wash the day off me. Once prepped and moisturized I pull out a gold silky dress and finish the look off with black heels and silver accessories. Applying a thin layer of make-up and rubbing my lips together to coat my lips evenly in a light red lipstick, I was done.

Grabbing my bag, I run for the door and hop into the waiting taxi. I said I would meet the girls there to save us all going back and forth on ourselves. We were dotted over London; I was more Kensington end.

We decided on Park Chinois, yes it was pricey, but we always went all out on our birthdays.

While I was riding in the taxi, I looked at the dating app on my phone to see an inbox full of messages. Swiping to delete most of them my eyes fell to a message that piqued my interest.

Shane

I furrowed my brows as I tapped on his message.

Hello HoppyMagnet123

Please don't take my message as anything more than a friendly reach out. I decided to give this dating app thing a go. Not that I've had much luck, and I am assuming that as you're on here that you haven't had much luck either. My wife cheated on me with my best friend, and to say my ego was hurt is an understatement. My family and friends have told me I need to get back in the saddle and stop wallowing. I'm not looking for anything romantic, I don't think…

My heart hurt for him.

No, no, I do not want a relationship; I just want some fun, a friend, companionship. I don't even know if this message will reach you but if it does, and you are willing to meet for a coffee and chat, then I hope you reply.

Shane

I scoffed, but not out of disgust. This man had reached out to me to ask me to meet him for a drink because he was lonely. Okay, it wasn't the most flattering message and made me feel even more unattractive than I already felt but his message made me feel warm and fuzzy inside too. I slipped my phone back in my bag as we pulled up outside the restaurant. I would reply to him later on, maybe.

It might do me good to go out with someone just for companionship rather than a relationship because clearly, I can't do relationships.

Paying the taxi driver, I climbed out of the car and walked towards the restaurant. Hopefully the girls were already in there so I wouldn't be sitting alone with my thoughts for too long.

The maître d' took my name and showed me to the table that had balloons sitting in the centre. There were two bottles of champagne sitting on ice and of course, my girls. Mabel, Tia and Hallie.

They all beamed at me, standing from their chairs and hugging me one by one.

"Oh, girls, you didn't have to go to this effort."

"I know we didn't," Hallie smiled, "but we wanted too."

"Well thank you, it's appreciated." I nod, sitting down and watching as Tia popped the champagne. She poured everyone a glass but herself. She was on water.

"How are you feeling?" I asked Tia as she took her seat next to me.

"Yeah, not too bad, a little sicky but hoping that'll pass in a few weeks. I'm halfway next week so if doesn't go then, I don't know when it will." She sighed as her hands rubbed softly over her bump.

"Hopefully not too much longer," I gave her a weak smile before looking at Hallie.

"And how are you, beautiful?" I asked. Her blonde hair shiny and thick as it sat in bouncy curls.

"I am okay, we start our next round of IVF in a couple of weeks so send me lots of baby dust and keep your fingers crossed." She smiled at us all.

"I'll send you baby dust, but keep it away from me," Mabel scoffed as she took a mouthful of her wine. I frowned, my brows pinching. I loved all my friends, but Mabel was sometimes a little harsh and insensitive towards the others at time. She was judgemental, but she was also a really good friend. Her timing just wasn't as good.

"Mabel..." I fired her daggers.

"What?" She shrugged, bringing her glass to her lips and draining the whole glass before reaching for the bottle.

"It's fine," Hallie let out a fake laugh, a smile spreading across her lips before quickly falling. Her façade slipping just as quickly as it came on.

I needed to get off the topic and get Hallie out of her head.

"So, I had a message on a dating app."

All their eyes pinned to me, and I felt my cheeks flush. Reaching for my champagne I took a mouthful to wet my lips.

"But not from a hoppy." I swallowed hard.

They said nothing.

"From a guy who has been cheated on, asking me if I would like to meet him for a little bit of companionship, and I sat and thought why the fuck not. He doesn't just want to get into my knickers, he won't be doing any bed hopping. He is lonely and his family have put him on a dating app." I laughed, the realisation of what I just said hitting me like a freight train. "I can't get a date, I can't hold down a relationship, so I mean, what have I got to lose? Really? Tell me? Me and Shane can be friends."

And they all just stare. They all look at me as if I have lost it. And do you know what? I think I may have.

"You are joking, right?" Tia asked, her eyes finally dragging from mine and moving to Mabel before they swept over to look at Hallie. Hallie met Tia's gaze, her mouth moving but no words coming out.

"And while I am making big decisions, my vagina is now closed for business..."

We were interrupted when the young male waiter approached the table, his eyes widening in horror at my vagina outburst.

I rubbed my lips together before a chuckle escaped me which made him laugh softly.

"What can I get you ladies?" He beamed.

Dinner was delicious. Walking arm in arm we headed deeper into the city, the streets were busy and trying to get a taxi was impossible. Heading down the steps to the tube station, I was standing with the girls waiting for our train, there was a rowdy group of men standing a little way from us, I couldn't keep my eyes from gravitating over towards them. I smiled, watching them be so carefree and laughing.

Hallie hooked her arm through mine as the wind blew down the station tunnels, a chill smothering me in goosebumps.

"Can I get your number?" The deep voice breezes over my skin, turning to face him I lift my brows.

"Bold and forward, aren't you?" I smirk, turning my attention back to Hallie.

"Look, if you don't ask you don't get." He shrugs his

shoulders up then looks over at his friends who are all sniggering.

"Are you on dating apps?"

I gasp, "Never you mind!" I laugh with him.

"Just tell me your name, come on, make me happy," he pleads, nudging into me.

Rolling my eyes, I look at Mabel and Hallie who are ushering me to tell him.

"It's Cody."

"Cody, I like it." He repeats after me and raises his eyebrows as if pleasantly surprised by how easily it rolls and feels on his tongue.

"I'm glad," I laugh, "and yours?"

"Nope, you'll find out if I find you on here." He waves his phone up at me showing the dating app.

"Good luck with that buddy, I don't go under my real name," I wink as our train pulls in.

"Oh what!" He calls out as we head towards the train doors, "you don't play fair!"

My head tips back and I giggle again as I step on the train, the doors closing behind me.

"He's cute!" Hallie says as we sit down.

"He is, isn't he." I agree, my smile widening.

I see Mabel's eyes widen as she looks out the window. "Erm, Cody... look out the window."

I turn slowly to look behind me to see my new stranger friend holding up his phone to the window, showing me my dating profile. The colour drains from my face.

"Oh fuck," I mouthed.

He's smiling, holding his thumb up then begins to wave as the train pulls away from the station.

Fuck it.

Chapter Three

THE ALCOHOL THAT WE HAD CONSUMED OVER DINNER
had hit me. I felt tipsy. All classiness that we had when we
were in the restaurant was now non-existent. Tia rolled her
eyes as she pushed us into the waiting black cab, the driver
giving as a tsk as we clamber in. Mabel's feet were hurting,
and she wasn't up for the ten minute walk to the club.

"Are you sure you don't want to come with us?" I whine
as she slams the door on us.

I press the button for the window, letting it slip down
slightly and hooking my fingers over the edge of glass.
"Absolutely positive," she smiles sarcastically. "Message me
when you all get home, enjoy the rest of your birthday,"
blowing me a kiss, she gets into the taxi behind ours.
Slumping back in my seat, I pout.

"She's a boreeeee," Mabel sighs as she taps on her
phone.

"She isn't a bore," Hallie snaps, "she is pregnant; just
hush, please, you're annoying me."

Mable flips her off and goes back to her phone. I just
shake my head from side to side and close my eyes for a

moment as the taxi pulls away from the kerb. My mood is suddenly dampened by the girls bickering.

"Girls, I might just go home," I click my tongue on the roof of my mouth. Mabel and Hallie's eyes both meet mine.

"No! It's your birthday! I need this night, pleaseeeee," Mabel begs, tossing her phone into her little clutch.

"Exactly, *you* need this night," Hallie slams her. I shake my head and fiddle with my bag.

"This is exactly why I want to go home," I snap.

"I'm sorry," Mabel exhales heavily, "I'm just, ugh," she shakes her head from side to side.

"Sorry too, let's go and have a good night yeah?" Hallie's voice is soft as her head dips to look at me.

I sigh.

"Fine, but no more bickering." I sulk, they're annoying me. My mood lifts when we pull outside the heaving club. *Cirque Le Soir.* I've heard amazing things about this place, but this is the first time we have ever been here. I spin round in my seat to look at Mabel.

"How?! The wait list for this place is huge!"

She winks and taps the side of her nose, "Never you mind," her smile growing.

Paying for the cab we tumble out the car, I head towards the line when I feel her hand wrap around mine as she tugs me back towards them.

"No waiting, we're VIP baby." She shouts as she toddles towards the doorman in her high heels. All my anger and tension soon slips away as the bouncer lets us through the thick, red rope. Then it dawns on me, George. Of course. Mabel's husband used to be a doorman, but now he is a scout going to all the cities around the world's hottest club scenes to find the next best thing.

We're led to a booth away from the hustle and bustle

and over to the VIP area just to the side of the stage. My eyes widen as I take in my surroundings, this place is amazing. My senses tingle as a sparkler filled bottle of champagne makes its way to our table. This night is going to be epic.

After a fantastic show, we were out on the pavements of London heading to our next destination. My senses were in overdrive and my mind was still trying to catch up with what I had just experienced. Walking into a busy club down a little alley, I crinkled my nose. It smelt musky and I am sure my feet were sticking to the carpet, but we were too tipsy to care.

"What do you want to drink?" Hallie shouted over *Post Malone.*

"Vodka and Soda please," pressing my thumbs up to her, she nodded and walked towards the bar. Mabel found a high bar table with some stools tucked under and empty, dirty glasses on it. She had the look of pure disgust on her face.

"George would be livid if he came here... this isn't his scene."

I roll my eyes, "I know, but we all have to start somewhere, right?" I nudge her. "You're getting a little snobby in your old age," I wink.

She rolls her eyes so far in the back of her head as Hallie bounds over with our drinks.

"Cheers!" She shouts as *Britney* blasts through the speakers, we clink glasses and take a mouthful.

I dry heave, "What vodka is this!? It tastes like paint stripper," I scrape my tongue under my top teeth willing to pull the taste from it.

"Who's the snob now?" Mabel smirks as she sips on her own drink.

"Bitch."

After a few more drinks, the alcohol is happily swimming through my veins, we've moved to the dance floor leaving our drinks on our table along with my jacket. Hopefully we will still have a seat once we're finished dancing.

Usher – Oh My God begins and me and the girls lose it. We're taken straight back to our younger years when we used to club hop every weekend and dance till the early hours of the morning.

Giggling and panting we head back to our table and fall into our seats. "How did we used to do this all night? My feet are killing me," I groan, kicking my heels off and rubbing my tired feet.

"I have no clue," Hallie puffs, taking a swig of her drink.

"I feel okay," Mabel shrugs her shoulders up while jigging and jiving in her seat.

We fall into light chatter when a group of men approach us. I sit tall, avoiding eye contact and focusing on the girls in front of me. I didn't come out to go home with anyone tonight. Tonight, is about me, myself and I. And my girls of course.

"Ladies," his voice is low and gruff as it floats through my ears causing my skin to prickle.

"Married," Hallie and Mabel say in unison holding their hands up and showing off their beautiful, diamond rings. Three of the guys hold their hands up and show their wedding bands as well. The girls instantly relax.

The group of guys laugh before falling back into easy conversation and Mabel joins in while the one who was closest drapes his arm over the back of my chair. My brows sit high as I stare at Hallie, and she smirks. I take another mouthful of paint stripper and slowly turn my head to look at him. My breath catches as I drink him in.

It's *him.*

Station guy.

This time, I really, *really*, take him in.

He is tall, broad and hairy. *Hairy!?* I internally scoff.

I let my eyes wander for a little longer, just to appreciate him. His eyes are light, crystal blue, with specks of grey dotted in. He has a neatly kept short beard. A mop of dark hair sits messy, and I can't help but wonder if it's intentionally messy or just him being lazy. I feel his eyes on me as I let mine continue down his body. Both his arms covered in full sleeve tattoos from his wrist up. Damn, he is broad. Like really broad. His white t-shirt is stretched across his large chest and clings a little round his stomach. It looks solid, he is thick, bulky, heavy set. *Dad bod.* That's the first thought that pops into my mind.

"Finished?" He asks, my eyes instantly moving back to his and I feel my cheeks burn with embarrassment that I have been caught checking him out. I nod, feeling suddenly bold and take another swig of my drink and wincing as I do.

"Do you come here often?" He asks as he drinks his beer and I laugh out loud.

"Wow, what a chat up line..." I giggle as I slowly turn my body to face him and now it's his turn to look me up and down. His eyes stay on my face for a while, as if he is trying to remember every feature. I feel like I've stopped breathing. How can this feel so intimate, my stomach knotting as I clench myself. What is wrong with me? His eyes fall to my heaving chest and his brows pop in appreciation, then he gives the rest of me one last sweep over. He winks at me and steps closer.

"I am the king of cheesy chat up lines and dad jokes, think it's best to just get that out there before we go any further so if cheese ball isn't your thing, then let me know and I'll crash and burn back onto the dancefloor." He smiles at me, and I smile back at him. He is not my type. I don't like guys like this, but this guy... I don't know... he seems different. *Maybe this is what I need. Different. Break the mould.*

"Cheese ball isn't my thing... but..." I smirk, "it is my birthday, so I am willing to go against the grain and give you a chance."

"Your birthday?! No way," he holds his beer bottle out for me to clink, "happy birthday," he says softly as we touch glasses. "I've got something other than birthday candles that you can blow..."

"Oh my god!" I slam my glass on the table and burst into laughter, "you're disgusting," I shove my hand into the top of his arm to shove him and it's solid. My fingertips tingle and I pull them away as quickly as I can. His body shakes as he chuckles with me.

"Okay, my bad. I should at least tell you my name before I ask you to blow me..." I roll my eyes.

"I'm Crew." He stands a little taller, his broad chest puffed out slightly. Silence rumbles through us for a moment, "and you are Cody right? Because, I don't think *Hoppymagnet*123 is your legal name."

"You remembered. Yeah, I'm Cody." I roll my lips.

"Cody and Crew." He mumbles out loud, "we sound like a cheesy duo with them names."

I hear Mabel cough and my head snaps to face them, my eyes widening. I was so immersed in Crew that I forgot about the girls.

"Oh my, how rude of me," I press my hand to my forehead, "I was so engrossed in us..." I blush.

"I have that effect on women." Crew shrugs his shoulders up nonchalantly, a cheeky grin pulling at the corners of his lips.

"Jeez, calm down. Your head will continue to grow, and you won't fit out the door," I tsk at him.

"Mabel, Hallie, this is Crew. Crew, Mabel and Hallie."

Crew holds his hand up and I can't help but notice the size of them, Jesus. They're big.

"Nice to meet you," Hallie smiles, "we've already met your mates," she thumbs behind her.

"Well, I haven't," I roll my lips as I sit and wait for Crew to introduce me.

"Willy, Dick and Harry," he gestures his hand to me, "please meet the birthday princess, Cody."

Mabel's eyes widen as she chokes on the drink she just inhaled and Hallie bursts into laughter.

"Shut up, you're such a clown." I elbow him hard in the ribs and chew on the inside of my cheek.

"What? I'm telling the truth!" He places the bottle on the table and walks around to his friends, standing next to each one. "This is Willy. Short for William," he raises his eyebrows as if I should know that already. "And this is Dick. Short for Richard," he smirks, and my cheeks flush red, "you dirty girl, you." He moves to the smaller guy at the end and whacks him on the back, "and this is Harry. There's nothing else, just Harry." He shrugs his shoulders up, his hand squeezing Harry's shoulder in a comforting way.

"Well, William, Richard and Harry, it's nice to meet you," I smile.

"Nope, sorry. They only respond to Willy and Dick," he smirks, his shoulders shaking as a light chuckle ripples through him, before taking a swig of his beer.

"I am not calling your friends that," I scowl at him, my lips pursed.

"Why? They like it."

"Oh piss off." I laugh and hop off the bar chair. "I'm popping to the ladies, girls?"

"Nah, we're okay here," they wave me away as they listen to Crew's friends talking.

"Oh," I nibble my bottom lip and reach for my clutch bag.

"It's okay, I'll come with you princess." He rolls his eyes and places his bottle back down on the table. "I need to touch my lipstick up anyway."

Chapter Four

Coming out of the toilets, I stand in front of the basins and wash my hands, smiling to myself. I wasn't looking for anyone or anything tonight other than to have a good time with my friends for my Birthday. Enter Crew. He was a breath of fresh air, and I welcomed him. Sure, he was a little cheesy and not what I would usually go for, but for some reason he made me feel safe. Shaking my hands out, I look around for a hand dryer but couldn't see one.

My vision blurred slightly. Shaking my head from side to side, I suddenly felt rough, my head pounded and felt as if it was trapped in a tight vice. My heart rate spiked and began beating fast, skipping beats as it did which made me catch my breath and gasp. I had perspiration beading on my forehead, I felt clammy and hot but then suddenly I was cold. My trembling hands turned the tap head, and I heard the water knocking around in the pipes, banging until the water spurted out of the tap head, it spurted out as I cupped my hands under the running water then splashed it over my face. It didn't help. I began panicking, my eyes widening as I felt the room begin to spin. My eyes were moving in one direction, but my head was moving in the opposite direction. I felt like I was on the old fairground ride, *the waltz*. My stomach churned and turned as I stepped away from the basin, losing my footing and sliding down the wall.

"Crew," I tried to call out, "Crew," but it was useless. My pleas just fell onto deaf ears. I fiddled around in my bag and pulled out my phone. I was seeing double. Tapping on Hallie's number, I couldn't even bring it to my ear before I called out for help and my world went black.

———

MY EYES STRUGGLED TO OPEN, THE BRIGHT LIGHT THAT shone through the room hurt my eyes. I squinted and pulled the duvet over my face. The panic swam through my veins as I realised I wasn't in my own bed. Looking down at my body, I was wearing a large, oversized t-shirt and boxer shorts. I swallowed the dry lump that was lodged in my throat. Peeling the covers back slowly, my eyes scanned the room. The bedroom was clean, it smelt homely, and wafts of coffee and vanilla swarmed the room. The top of the wall was a deep navy and the bottoms under the dado rail was white. It broke the room up, making it feel airy and making the room look a lot bigger than it was. I tried to find anything that would give me a hint of where I was and who I was with but there was nothing. I heard the creak of the door, nerves unsettled me and I got back under the duvet and pulled it up and over my head and hoped for the best. What the fuck happened to me last night? I know I was drunk but I wasn't black out drunk!

To be honest, when I met Crew, I felt like he sobered me up. The anxiety crashes through me and it makes me feel sick to the pit of my stomach. *Oh my god, the girls!* Footsteps approach and I can hear my heart jack hammering, pounding into the flesh of my chest, the sickly heavy beating drowning my ears.

The end of the bed dipped. This was it. I was going to meet the person who was going to murder me. Silencing my breathing, I inhaled deeply and held my breath. The cover was snatched back and that's when I saw him.

"Hey," he smiled down at me, his messy hair all over the place, his blue eyes glistening as they stayed on mine.

"Oh thank Christ," I cry out, my heart ricocheting. Throwing my arms around his neck and holding onto him.

"Easy tiger," the playfulness was evident in his voice. "I take it this means you're pleased to see me?"

I pull away from him and nibble on my bottom lip as he slips into bed next to me. I take this moment to admire him. Sure, I gave him a good eye fuck last night but he was now next to me and only wearing black cotton shorts. His broad and solid chest was scattered in a dusting of dark brown hair, covering most of his chest area then running in a neat line all the way down to his waistband and into his shorts. He had small, random tattoos dotted over his skin, two on his chest, and two full sleeves. They reminded me of my late grandad and the types of tattoos he had. Meaningful to him, but to the outside world, they were *just* tattoos.

My tongue darted out quickly as I licked my upper lip. His stomach had a slight round to it, but he suited the build. He was a real man, and I was turned on by him. I had slept with a few Ken Barbie dolls in my days and something about Crew was so much hotter and appealing to me than them.

"Very pleased to see you," I breathe out in relief. "What the fuck happened to me last night? All I remember is you walking to the toilet with me, I washed my hands and then everything went black."

"Yeah, then I had Hallie, I think that's her name..." he pauses for a moment, "yeah, that's her name. Willy had a raging boner all night," he shook his head, "anyway, she came running towards me asking where I was and that you had called her, but she couldn't make heads or tails of what you were going on about."

A gasp leaves me.

"And why did you bring me home? Why didn't my *friends* take me home?" I asked with bite, it stung.

"They offered, but I insisted on bringing you back here so I could make sure you were okay..."

One of my brows raise.

"You do realise how creepy that makes you sound right?" I smirk, slowly edging away from him, taking the duvet with me.

"Damn it, you're on to me. I was hoping to lock you in my bedroom forever," he wiggles his brows at me and somehow, he eases my anxiety.

"I don't know what happened, I wasn't that drunk... I know when I have had too much and sure, I had inhaled a lot, but I was pretty sober by the time I met you," I continued my ramble, "I suppose I drunk myself sober," I shrug my shoulders up and smiled weakly.

"You weren't drunk..." his silly, playful mood quickly slipped, "you were spiked."

"I was what?!" I hissed, and suddenly the penny drops. "Was this part of a sick plan? Was you planning on date raping me!?"

"Oh my god," he booms, his beautiful blue eyes widening in shock. "Are you fucking shitting me? Why would I spike your drink?"

I said nothing, because truthfully, I felt shit for even asking and doubting him. The uneasiness sinks deep into my stomach.

"I'm..." I stammer and he inhales deeply.

"Cody, I didn't spike you. I had been watching you all night, I was drawn to you for some unknown reason. But you left your drink on your table, open for anything to go into it. You need to be more responsible. What if I hadn't been there? What if whoever done it managed to get you back home? Honestly, the stories I hear in work about the girls and the men who get drugged while out..." his voice trails off as his eyes fall to his lap.

"I'm sorry," I mumble, my voice barely audible. I felt awful.

"It's fine, I mean, you don't really know me, do you?" He shrugs his heavy, broad shoulders up as if not bothered but I can see how much it has bothered him that I made that accusation.

Silence cripples us for a while, neither of us saying anything until the smoke alarm rips through the apartment, making us both jump.

"Fuck, the bacon," he groans, scrambling out of bed and running down the hallway.

I slip back down the bed and giggle as he darts out the door. Silly man.

I sat alone and let Crew's words play over on repeat in my head, what a bitch I was for accusing him. But then again, I didn't know him, so it wasn't overly bad that I thought of that. I was ripped from my thoughts when I heard a creak on the floorboards. Crew walked back in with two cups of coffee and sat on the edge of the bed next to me, handing me my cup.

"I burnt breakfast," the corner of his lip lifted, his eyes falling to his cup.

"I figured by the smoke alarm," I shrugged my shoulder up as I brought the cup to my lips and took a mouthful as I tried to contain my smile.

He tapped his large, thick fingers on the side of the china cup.

"Crew..." I say quietly, his head snaps up as he looks at me. "I am sorry for accusing you..." my cheeks pinch crimson.

"I know," he nods, "I get it, I do, you don't know me from Adam, and you woke up in my bed without remembering how you got there."

I nod and take another mouthful. My mind wanders to the girls and my gut aches. I sit forward and it's as if Crew knows what I am thinking.

"I messaged the girls as soon as we were home last night, your phone is on charge just down the side of the unit there," he points to the bedside unit. Reaching down I pull it out and find Hallie's number. "I'll leave you be, I washed your dress last night. I'll iron it and lay it out. Shower is just through that door next to my wardrobe." He smiles. Before I could say anything he was gone, closing the door behind him.

My finger hovered over Hallie's name for a moment before I gave in and clicked dial.

Ring.

Ring.

Ring.

"Cody!?" She screeched down the phone. I winced, pulling the phone from my ear and putting her onto speaker.

"Hey," I said a little sheepishly, picking at the skin round the nails of my fingers.

"Are you okay? Shit Cody, I have been so anxious all night and Crew was so amazing." She sighed heavily.

"I'm fine, head is a little heavy but that's to be expected. I don't get how it happened." I shake my head from side to side.

"Neither do I, but you get scum who think it's okay to do this. I am just so glad Crew, and his friends were there."

Silence brews between us, butterflies swarming my stomach. I loved that feeling.

"I accused Crew of spiking me." I burst out, and face palm my face, the guilt eating me alive.

"Oh Cody."

"I know, Hallie, I feel awful," I whisper now.

"I get it though," she says sweetly, "anyone would get it, but honestly Cody you have nothing to worry about when it comes to Crew. He is a good one, I can feel it."

"I can feel it too. Something about him isn't there..." I trail off. "Hallie?" I ask.

"Yup."

"Am I on speaker phone?"

"No, why?"

"I heard Dick had a raging boner for you all night," I snigger as I flop back against the headboard.

"Oh, for goodness sake, stop it," she laughs.

"I thought he was married?"

I hear her sigh.

"He is, but from what he was saying last night their marriage is going down the shitter..."

"Lovely use of words there my love." I roll my eyes, "that's a shame though, kids?"

"Yeah, one," her voice is quiet, and the line falls silent.

"Your time will come," I say softly, knowing just how much she wants to be a mum, both her and Derek are desperate to be parents.

"I know hun, but I have been thinking…" she stalls for a moment, and I wait. "I think this is going to be my last round. I can't keep going through this, the three times I have fallen I have lost them. I'm just not meant to carry a baby." The crack in her voice pulls on my heart strings, I wish I could do something to help them.

"Hallie, please…" I was practically begging her, "please don't give up."

"I don't have any more fight left in me," her voice was barely audible and for some reason I felt like she wasn't just talking about her conceiving journey.

"Hals," I sigh, "let's do lunch later."

"Maybe, babes, I have to go… I'll message in a bit, I'll let the other two know that you're awake and okay."

"Thanks hun, love you."

"Love you," the phone cuts off. I inhale deeply and stare at the door. I need to shower. I stink.

Once showered, I walk back to the bedroom with the towel pulled tightly round my body and smile when I see my gold dress on the bed.

I trace my fingers over the material before looking at the clothes that are bunched in my other hand. Is it wrong that I want to put Crew's clothes back on? My skin prickles then anxiety punches me in the gut that he undressed me last night. My eyes widen.

No, no, no.

I sit on the edge of his bed just as he walks through the bedroom door.

"Crew," I say quietly.

"Cody?" his brows lift.

"Did you see me naked last night?" I blush.

"Maybe?" He winks and chuckles.

I face palm myself.

"Nahhh, just kidding princess. You undressed yourself. Not quite sure how you managed. I sat you on the bed to get a bowl because you were throwing up and when I returned you were in my clothes..."

"I'm so sorry." Ugh. I am mortified.

"Stop saying sorry. You have nothing to be sorry about."

I nod, rolling my lips together. I hear him sigh.

"Can we start this morning again? Get dressed and I'll take you for breakfast."

"That sounds perfect. But can we swing by mine, I don't fancy going out in my dress or your underwear..."

"Of course, we can," we smile at each other, "but I have on stipulation."

"And what is that?"

"You have to keep my underwear on," he wiggles his eyebrows at me, his fingers wrapping around the door. I rush forward and shove him out the bedroom and slam the door behind him. Pervert.

Chapter Five

I sit on the edge of my bed, Crew is standing in the doorway, his large frame leant against the door threshold. I feel sick to my stomach, nausea sweeping through me. Clamminess coats my skin, and my head begins to thump.

"Rainbow drop, are you okay?" His voice floats across the room, my chest hurts as my eyes find him.

"Rainbow drop?" My brows pinch.

"Not a fan?"

"No, not at all."

"Was that a 'no, not at all' to the nickname or was it answering my 'are you okay'?"

"Both," I snap, falling back on the bed. "Why do I feel so rough?" Groaning, I roll onto my side and move to the foetal position.

"Because you have drugs in your system, I'm sorry it happened to you," I hear his footsteps closing the space between us.

"All the years I have been out, I have never, ever been spiked."

"It only takes one time."

"We should have stayed in the city, serves me right for going into that dive of a bar."

"Baby cakes, it could have happened anywhere."

I turn my head to look at him over my shoulder.

"No."

"No?"

"That nickname," I hiss, "veto."

Silence crackles between us and I close my eyes for a moment. My whole body aches and I feel heavy as I sink into my mattress. Suddenly, my hair is brushed from my head and my skin tingles.

"Go and have another shower, you're dripping in sweat. I will stay here until you feel better, I don't want to leave you on your own."

My heart swells. How is he so sweet? I have never met anyone like him.

I nod slowly, rolling away from him and letting my feet hit the carpet. I watch as he moves from the bed, the frame moving as he shifts his weight. He moves towards the door before turning to face me, "Remember, singing in the shower is fun until you get soap in your mouth." His face serious, his eyes narrowing on me. I raise my brows, my lips twisting. "Then it's a soap opera." He smirks before turning on his heel and walking away.

I giggle softly and head towards my bathroom, praying I feel better after.

I am snuggled in my tracksuit, my brown hair still wet and scraped into a heap on the top of my head. I feel and look like death I am sure, yet for some unknown reason, Crew is still here. He hands me a cup of tea and two painkillers.

"Take them, they'll kill the headache a little." Holding my hand out he drops them into my hand. "You hungry?"

I shake my head from side to side and he nods and slips back into the kitchen. I sigh, this is not the way I expected my evening to go. Here I have this amazing and sweet guy and I feel like I am about to throw the contents of my stomach up at any minute. Everything just goes to shit when it comes to me and dating. He is here out of sympathy, as soon as I feel better, he will hop skip and jump out of that door just like all the other hoppys I meet, the only difference with Crew was that we didn't sleep together and for some reason I don't know whether I am disappointed or relieved.

Lost in my thoughts I don't even hear my front door open; my eyes are pinned to the television even though I have no idea what is playing.

"Is she alright?" I hear Mabel's voice hum past me.

"Yeah," Crew's gruffness coats my skin in prickles of goosebumps.

"Hey babe," Mabel crouches down in front of me, "how are you feeling?"

"Shit," I grunt, falling back onto the sofa and letting out a deep huff.

"We bought you food," she smiles sweetly as Hallie flops down next to me, Tia sitting on the other couch opposite me.

"I'm not hungry, I just feel too sick to my stomach to even think about food."

Mabel nods, standing slowly and taking the bag of food into the kitchen. Hallie wraps her arm around my shoulders.

"What a shitty way to spend your birthday aye," she scoffs, and I let out a little laugh

"I thought you said your birthday was yesterday?" Crew asks as he stands in front of me, pulling his lightweight navy jacket over his shoulders. *He's leaving?* I swallow the lump down that's lodged in my throat.

"It was, it had gone midnight when we met…" I scrunch my nose, "I think."

"I see," he licks his lips, his eyes burning through me, and I feel the scorch burn deep inside of me. He shifts from foot to foot, "I'm going to head out, I've got work later and have a few things to sort out. I've put my number in your phone, so if you need me, you can call me." He smiles softly, the corners of his beautiful blue eyes creasing slightly.

I nod.

"Thank you, Crew, honestly." My throat feels tight, "Not many men would have helped me the way you did."

"I'm not *many men*, Cody." He steps towards me and leans in, placing a gentle and soft kiss on my forehead. "See you around buttercup," his lips mutter across my skin then he inhales my scent before standing tall.

"Veto," I scowl, "I'm not a power puff girl." He chuckles softly then disappears down the hallway before the click of the door lets me and the girls know that he has gone. It's only then do I let out the breath I have been holding.

"Well…" Tia's brows raise in her forehead as a silly grin plays on her lips, Mabel sits her skinny bum on the arm of the sofa as all their eyes move to me.

"Well what?" I scoff as I take a mouthful of my now cold tea.

"You going to fill us in?" Mabel asks, her mouth agape, her tongue sitting at the corner of her lips.

"Nothing to fill you in on, nothing happened." I shrug my shoulders up, "The only thing that happened during my night was getting spiked and you already know that happened. You also know that Crew looked after me. There is nothing else to say."

"Will you call him?" Hallie asks, "Like, would you like to see him again?"

I hang on her question for a moment, my mind playing the last few hours over in my mind.

"I don't think so," I shake my head, "it was nothing more than what it was. A new friend looking out for another. He isn't attracted to me, I'm not attracted to him. Maybe we will be friends, but that's all it will be. I am still one hundred percent sticking to my vow last night, my vagina is closed to anyone but me and my toys and I am swearing off men for life. I have Dillan the dildo, I don't need anything or anyone else to make me orgasm." I nod as I stand slowly, I need to stretch.

"Dillan is the only *one* who makes you orgasm anyway," Tia rolls her eyes.

"And what does that mean?"

"You know what that means," Hallie narrows her eyes on me as she shuffles in her seat.

I stay silent

"When was the last time a dude got you off?"

"I can't remember." I shrug as if it wasn't a big deal, but in fact it was a massive fucking deal, and I am certain that is the reason these guys hop out of my bed. I am hard work. I'm not an easy lay. So, I let them get their selves off, fake a moan or two and then let them hop on their way. I am just over trying to make myself come for someone who does nothing for me.

"Exactly, but what if dreamy Crew is the one to hit your spot," Mabel winks, nudging Tia in the arm as she does.

"Dreamy Crew will be hitting none of my spots, thank you." I snap as I walk out the lounge leaving their cackles behind me.

But what if they were right? Crew isn't my type, well, I

didn't *think* he was my type but the way he makes me tingle in all the right places, making me feel anchored and grounded whenever he is close... and yet, I let him walk out without seeing if this had potential.

I am a screw up.

Always have been. Always will be.

Chapter Six

25th Birthday

We sit at the top of The Shard, clinking our glasses of prosecco together. "Happy Birthday, Cody!" The girls chime as we all take a sip.

"Thank you girls," I smile as I look out over the beautiful city below us, street lights and house lights twinkling like stars beneath.

"Anyone take your fancy?" Mabel asks, her eyes falling to her watch.

"Somewhere to be?" I ask her, licking my lips before a giggle leaves me.

"No! Just waiting for George to get off. He said he was going to meet us here," she sighs.

"I'm sure he will be here." I give her a reassuring smile. Mabel and George have been dating for the last three years, they're head over heels in love with each other. Tia is with her old high school crush and Hallie has just started dating a stockbroker called Derek.

And me? Well, it's just me and Dillan. My dildo.

"Is Derek coming?" I ask as I take another mouthful of my drink to wash down the bitter taste in my mouth.

"He is, he is bringing a couple of his friends..." Hallie stops, her eyes bugging out as she glares at me, "I hope you don't mind."

"Of course I don't," I smile, the hopeless romantic in me hopes he is my prince charming, my knight in shining armour.

We continue with our evening when I see Hallie's eyes widen with glee and excitement when she sees Derek approaching. He is tall, broad and really, bloody handsome. My eyes floated behind him to see two impeccably dressed and beautiful men walking into the restaurant. Derek kissed Hallie then stepped aside and kissed me on the cheek.

"Happy Birthday, Cody."

"Thank you," I blush as he steps back and wraps his arm around Hallie's waist.

"This is Alex and Otis," he smiles, his head turning back to his two friends who hold their glasses up at me.

Happy Birthday indeed.

STUMBLING THROUGH THE STUNNING PENTHOUSE THAT Otis owns, I kick my shoes off and lose my balance, but of course he is there to catch me.

"Thanks," I say breathless, his fingers sweeping my hair from my face as they trail down my cheekbone before gripping my chin. He edges his face closer, his lips brushing against mine and I swear I forget to breathe and just for a moment, time stands still.

"Let's go and get to know each other a little better," a devilishly handsome smirk pulls at his lip as he clasps my hand and leads me towards his bedroom.

Maybe there is such a thing as love at first sight.

THE NEXT MORNING, I ROLL OVER, MY HAIR A MESS AND *sleep still evident in my eyes. I let them roam over the naked god that lays next to me and my heart thumps.*

Trailing my fingers over his back in a tickling manner, he stirs and rolls over to face me.

"Morning," a small smile crosses my lips.

"Morning," he smiles, stretching and I continue to let my eyes travel.

"Last night was..." I nibble on the inside of my lip.

"It was something, right," his words are slow as he swings his legs off the bed and suddenly, the anxiety smacks me straight in the face. I know what is coming next.

"Do you wanna get some breakfast?" I ask, picking the skin round my nails.

"I can't today, I am swamped." He gives me a sorry shrug of his shoulders and begins to collect his scattered clothes off the floor and heads into a bathroom, the door slamming shut. I still, my mouth agape and my eyes wide. The bathroom door opens slightly, and his head pops out.

"If you wouldn't mind leaving, I've got to get moving as soon as I am ready."

I swallow the thickness down in my throat, my eyes pricking with tears but I won't let them fall.

"Sure," I nod, moving from the bed and grabbing my clothes from the floor. Otis says nothing, just gives me a curt nod then slams the door once more.

This is the last time I am coming to someone's house; I can't cope with the humiliation anymore.

I burst through his penthouse door and fly for the lift, embarrassment tarnishes me as I run out the building as quick as I can. Humiliation floods me and as soon as I am outside, I let my tears fall, the pouring down rain camouflaging my upset. I lift my arm to hail a cab and don't look back.

Screw you, Otis.

Chapter Seven

Crew

Present Day

I sit at lunch with Will, Rich and Harry, they're talking about last night and all I can think about is Cody. Sipping my beer, I hear Will call me.

"Crew?"

"Yeah bud?" I ask, my voice light as I pin my eyes to him.

"You okay?"

"Yeah, just tired. Buzz has gone," I laugh, "it was a long night."

"You dirty old dog," Will scoffs, taking a sip of his own beer.

"Not like that." I shake my head, my brows pinching as I feel irritation beginning to bubble inside of me. "She got fucking spiked man, I'm not a prick. I wouldn't sleep with her unconscious, Jesus Christ." Pushing my hand through my dark hair in frustration.

"Woah, man I was just kidding," his eyes widen as he looks at our other two friends who hang their heads.

"I'm sorry mate, I'm just tired. I feel all twisted up and wired inside." I chew the inside of my cheek.

"They were fun weren't they?" Rich says as he stabs his fork into his chips.

"Yeah they were," I admit, "I can't believe she got fucking spiked man, I am more pissed off that she let it happen."

"Sometimes they have to learn the hard way," Harry shrugs his shoulders up, "I don't mean that in a cunty way or anything. Just some girls think they're safe from anything like that happening, we all know the horror stories from work and the date rape drug," he clenches his jaw. "People are fucking scum, prying on a group of girls." Shaking his head from side to side in disappointment.

"You're right, when I see her again I'll have to give her a little lesson in what to do when she next goes out."

"So, you're going to see her again," Rich smirks, eyeing the guys.

"Hopefully," I shrug my shoulders up in a nonchalant way. I don't want to seem desperate. But truth was, I was fucking desperate. I was craving her and I only left her just over an hour ago. Me and my friends meet every Saturday if we can, and us going out last night was a rarity. I needed to let off some steam and we wanted to get Will out because of his cunt of a wife. I continue to chew the inside of my cheek.

"What if she doesn't want to see you?"

"Then I leave her be, I'm not some possessive, obsessive wanker." I snort, picking my sandwich up.

"You won't leave her be," Will laughs as he holds his hand up to order another round of beers.

"Not for me mate, I've got work shortly," I state, shaking

my head. "I'll have a coffee," I chime to the waitress, and she nods.

"We all know that when you get into work you'll start looking into her background."

"Oh behave, no I won't."

And with that, the table erupts into laughter.

"Anyway, knob rot, enough about me, you were getting a little close with her friend last night... fuck, what was her name?"

"Hallie," Will grits out.

"Ah, yes, Hallie. You know you're married right?" I smirk, I love winding him up. His wife is a monster, treats him like absolute shit. We have never liked her but tolerated her for his sake. Best thing she could do was to break his heart. As horrible as that may sound, he needs it. Because that will be the only reason he would contemplate leaving her and the life he has become so accustomed to.

"Fuck off," he growls as he passes the waitress his empty beer bottle and swaps it out for a full one. I hear the sigh leave him. "We just got on. It's one of them, right person, wrong time."

My eyes widen slightly.

"You literally just met her," I choke out.

"When you know, you know," he shrugs his shoulders up before draining his beer.

Well fuck.

WORK IS LONG AND HONESTLY; I AM FUCKING WIPED. I hardly slept last night, I couldn't take my eyes off her. I wish it was just out of fear, but it wasn't. I was besotted with her. My mind floats back to last night with her laying in my bed.

Her thick, long brown hair was tucked under her. I tried my best to get her make-up off, but I am no pro. I feel the blood rush to my cock as I think back to how my large grey tee clung to her curves, the hem sitting just over her hips revealing her pale skin. I wanted to kiss her there, leave a small mark but I couldn't. I had to make sure she was okay, to protect her. My chest ached and I don't know why. Maybe it was the thought that I left her when I didn't want to, but I didn't know her. Fuck, I knew her name and where she lived. If I wanted to, I could type her name into my system but that's a little fucked up. I scoff. Okay. It's a lot fucked up.

Tapping the screen on my phone I see a blank screen. My brows furrow and I inhale deeply, I thought she would have messaged by now. *Did I read it wrong?*

"Mann, you ready? We've got a call."

I sigh, shutting the screen off on my computer and pushing out.

"Yup, where are we heading?"

"Noise complaint."

I roll my eyes. "I am so glad I spent copious years in training to attend fucking noise complaints."

"Tell me about it," Paddy groans as we head towards our car. I have been working my bollocks off to get promoted into the undercover side of things, dealing with bigger jobs than fucking noise complaints.

"Who's driving?" Paddy asks.

"Rock, paper, scissor it?"

Paddy huffs, "Fine."

"One, two, three," I call.

I present a rock, he presents scissors.

"Sucker," I laugh, snatching the keys from his grasp and heading towards the *BMW X5*.

"You can get the food for that you cocky fuck."

I chuckle, "Okay, I'll treat you to a happy meal," winking, I climb in the car and start the engine.

MY HEART THUMPS WHEN I PULL DOWN THE STREET, nibbling the inside of my lip to stop the smirk.

"Here it is, 69," Paddy says, clicking his radio to tell the operator that we're here.

Pulling into the space just outside her house, I swallow. Why do I feel nervous?

I look up at the end terrace house, the blinds are drawn but I can hear the music thumping. *Her headache must've gone. That's good.*

Stepping up towards her front door, I smirk as I hit the gold knocker. We wait but nothing.

"Some party," Paddy smiles.

"Mm," I hum as I knock a little louder this time. Instantly, the music dies, and I see a figure approach the door.

I swallow, my palms sweaty as the front door swings open, her mouth gapes and her eyes widen.

"Hello, you," I croon, my hands crossed as I lean against the wall in her porch.

"*Crew,*" she hisses, her eyes pinned to mine.

"Honeybun."

"Veto."

"Spoil sport."

"So, you know her then?" Paddy's brow pings high into his forehead.

"Not really," I shrug.

"Why are you here?" She crosses her arms across her full chest. I try not to let my eyes fall, but I can't help it. My eyes rake up and down her body and my body reacts. She has a red tight dress wrapped round her curves and it sits mid-thigh. Her long, thick legs are toned and all I can think about is how much I want them wrapped round my face as I fucking devour her. Her brown hair is sitting in loose curls and frames her face perfectly, letting me see her beautiful fucking eyes.

"Noise complaint," Paddy answers, clearly aware of my inability to speak.

"Are you fucking serious?" She scowls, stepping forward and looking at her neighbour's house. "Fucking Gary."

"This is normal then?" I ask, snapping back into the present.

"Yeah, he is a lonely moron who has nothing better to do on a Saturday night. He probably sits and jerks off over the police officers that come here," she rolls her eyes in an overexaggerated manner.

"I see." I tense, *fucking Gary.*

Paddy pulls his notepad out. "Look, no doubt peeping Tom is watching out the window, so I am going to do some scribbles, maybe draw a picture, but just keep it down a little yeah?"

She nods, "sure," her eyes bat to the floor and she looks at her feet. They're sitting in high black heeled pumps. My cock swells at the thought of fucking her with just them on.

"I'll give you a minute, Mann." Paddy nods his head gently then walks away to the car.

"So, a police officer aye..." she smirks at me, her eyes rolling up and down my body.

"Yup," I wink. The air crackles between us, my breath snatched as I take her in.

"Are you feeling better?" I step closer to her, my eyes volleying back and forth between hers.

"Much better. Had a long nap after you left and was force fed some food," The corners of her mouth lift.

"Force feeding your thing?"

"No," she scoffs.

"I'm glad you're feeling better sugar plum."

"Where do you get these from!?" She laughs, tipping her head back, "Veto."

"Damn it, I really thought you would have taken to that one."

"Nope."

Silence again. I cough and clear my throat.

"Okay, well, I'll let you enjoy your night." I step away and for the first time the pull tugs me back like an uncontrollable force, but I must resist. I can't. We can't. It's not like that.

"Okay," she smiles at me and lingers.

Walk away Crew.

"See ya around," I hold my hand up, giving her a half smile before finally turning and walking towards the car. I can't look back.

I let out the breath I was holding when I get back into the car.

"Wanna talk?" Paddy asks as he puts his phone away.

"Nope."

"Okay," he sighs.

The rest of the journey was silent. I was just alone with my thoughts.

I sit spinning in my chair at my desk, the night is slow. I hate the nights like this. I am on till three am and I am already flaking. My eyes move to the slow ticking clock on the wall, *tick tock, tick tock, tick tock.*

It's just gone eleven-thirty and I am bored out of my skull; all I can think about is Cody in that red dress.

Paddy appears with a large coffee and slice of Victoria sponge.

"This will do wonders for my figure," the sarcasm dripping from my tongue as I pat my stomach. "Don't wanna ruin my six pack."

Paddy throws his head back and laughs, squeezing my shoulder.

"I have never known you to have a six pack," he teases.

"And I wouldn't want one. Fuck that. All of them hours wasted down the gym when I can be sitting here with all of this crime and cake. Who would wanna miss out on this," I grin as I take a mouthful of my black coffee.

Sure, would I like to be a little trimmer? A little less wobbly in places? Of course. But I wasn't built that way. I was solid, bulky, hefty. I was large. Always have been. I was always the bigger, tall, tubby boy at school. I had just filled out more now, yes, I worked out but only for my health. I wasn't interested in changing my physique. I am who I am. I'm curvy and I'm happy.

The hours slip by slowly and I finally give into temptation. I type her address and name in and there she is.

Cody Kempner.

Chapter Eight

Cody

IT'S SUNDAY AND I AM HANGING OUT MY ARSE. I DON'T know why I do it to myself. I've got to stop. It's too much and I am far too old now. I scroll through socials and catch up while I have *Selling Sunset* playing in the background to drain the silence out. Opening my many dating apps I see a few creeps that have lurked on my profile, turning my nose up I find Shane's message and re-read it. All of these men on these dating apps and I am messaging an old man about meeting for coffee. Shoot me now.

Smiling, I begin to type.

> Shane,

> Thank you so much for reaching out to me. How very kind of you. I love that your family are trying to get you back on the horse as such. I hope we can be friends.

> I would love to meet for coffee, you just let me know a time and a place and I'll be there.

> Thanks for reaching out, I look forward to hearing from you soon.

> Cody

I send the message then lock the screen of my phone. I lay staring at the ceiling, my eyes pinned. My thoughts are consumed with Crew. Every second of today I have thought about him. Part of me wants to text him, but then I don't think he wants me to because if he did, he would have taken my number. I huff, pulling myself up from the sofa. I log onto my computer and open my work schedule. I am back-to-back for most of the week which I like, it makes my days go quicker but I just cannot be bothered. I'll be fine once I am there and lost in my work but at the moment, I feel like booking a weekend away and escaping for a while.

My phone dings and my heart jumps up into my throat.

One message on my dating app. Realisation anchors my heart back down into my chest knowing it's Shane.

My fingers hover over my keys, Crew's partner called him Mann which I am assuming was his last name. I contemplate searching him, but I decide against it. I am becoming obsessive, it's ridiculous.

My phone buzzes and it's Hallie. I smile.

"Hey, you okay?"

"Yeah, yeah, are you?"

"Yup," I blow my cheeks full of air before drawing it out slowly.

"Fancy the races next weekend? I know you're mega busy because of wedding season but I need out for a bit."

I open my laptop again and go through my work diary, "Possibly, I will see if one of the girls will cover with my mum. It's gonna be a push though 'cause I had this weekend covered." I sigh.

"Just close shop, you're the boss."

"Ha!" I scoff, "if only it was that easy."

"Mm," she hums.

"Are the others coming?" I ask.

"Of course, of course. Mabel is packing her suitcase already; we all seem pretty desperate."

"That we do," I agree but my mind is elsewhere because all I think about is Crew. Jesus, this is depressive. What the fuck is wrong with me.

"You still there?"

"Yeah, just daydreaming."

"About a certain bulky guy…"

"No," I snap a little quicker than I should have, giving my lies away.

"Aha! I knew it."

"Oh, shut up, you know nothing," I smirk into the phone, my cheeks a blaze.

"I do," she sings.

"I'm horny that's all."

"Go and have fun with Dillan."

"You know what, I'm going to." The line falls silent, "I'll let you know about racing later," I smile then cut the phone off.

Rushing to my room, I shut the door and pull my little friend out. He knows how to hit the spot and it'll hopefully stop my mind from wandering to dreamy Crew.

I tsk at myself, I am like an addict chasing my next high. Damn it. He is swimming through my veins and invading my mind. I let my legs drop as I position my battery-operated friend right where I need him. The pleasure ripping through me like wildfire I let my lids flutter shut and as soon as they are I see Crew. His mouth on me, his blue eyes pinned to mine as I watch him lick and suck on my clit, his stubble marking me in the best way before he fills me with two thick fingers. I feel the burning knot in my stomach, my skin erupting as I feel my orgasm building. Slipping my toy inside of me, I stretch around it and rub my sensitive clit as I explode, Crew invading my thoughts as I ride it out.

I ping my eyes open, throwing Dillan on the bed as if he had just burned the most sensitive part of me.

"Fuck," I pant.

I reach for my phone and open a message to Hallie.

> I just got off to Crew.

I wait.

> I fucking knew it. Enjoy it, ask him out. You never know...

I read her message repeatedly, anxiety growing in my chest.

> I can't. He isn't into me.

> How do you know?

> I just do.

Dropping my phone, I move downstairs to the bright kitchen and start dinner. I need to keep my mind busy. Pulling the contents of my fridge out, I decide on a vegetable curry. My stomach groans in appreciation as the smell begins to waft through my nose, I suddenly felt famished.

Settling down in front of the tele and picking up where I left off with *Selling Sunset,* I pushed Crew to the back of my mind and that's where he would stay.

. . .

MONDAY MORNING WAS IN FULL FORCE AS I SAT
sweating in the back room. Even though the room had to
stay at a cooler temperature, my body didn't get the memo. I
was running round like a headless chicken trying to get
everything ready. We had a dusk wedding to set up
Wednesday morning and three weddings to prepare for this
weekend. My mum offered to cover and roped four of the
part time girls in promising them triple pay. I bit my tongue
at her offer because I didn't have a leg to stand on.

I was meeting Mabel and Tia for lunch; Hallie would
be missed as she had couples therapy this afternoon just like
she does every Monday. Walking onto the busy pavement,
we head towards *The Ivy*. The taxi pulls kerbside, and I pay
before the girls even have a chance. We're seated quickly
and our coffees are with us in no time. This is the first hot
drink I have had today so far. I was up and out nice and
early and then work had been keeping me busy which I was
grateful for.

"I am so over today," Tia groaned as she popped an olive
into her mouth.

"As am I, I hate Mondays."

"Well at least you get to go out and do something,"
Mabel groans as she tries to pacify Rocco. I give her a
sympathetic smile.

"Want me to take him?" I ask, holding my arms out and
smiling.

"No, it's fine. I need to try and get him to sleep, I can't
break his routine." My smile fades and I drop my hands
quickly.

"What can I get you ladies?" The server asks as he eyes
each of us.

"I'll have the prawn and avocado sandwich please."

"I'll have the same," Mabel says sweetly.

"And I'll have the haloumi burger please."

"Fabulous choices, I will get your order put in." He nods then turns and heads for the kitchen.

AFTER LUNCH, I DECIDE TO JUMP OUT WITH TIA AND have a slow walk back to my shop. The sun is shining, and my mind is too hectic with thoughts of Crew and it's driving me insane. I should just stop being stubborn and message him, but I feel like I am going to get hurt and I am too fragile to get hurt, or am I?

Pulling out my phone, I reluctantly open the dating app that pinged me last night. *Shane.*

We settled a date for coffee on Thursday morning at the shop. He said it wasn't far from him and he walks past it frequently on his walks with his dog. I'm lonely, but his loneliness is worse than mine. He lost the love of his life and is now living without her due to powers out of his control. I rub my chest to try and relieve the pain a little. Fumbling through my phone I scroll to C and don't see his name.

I frown, he said he put his number in my phone. I keep scrolling and then I see it.

Dreamboat.

I can't with this man. I giggle softly and toss my phone into my bag.

CLOSING THE SHOP, ME AND MY MUM HEAD TO THE back where she parks her car and I hop in. Monday night is lasagne night at my mum's, and I look forward to it every week.

Stumbling through the door, I toss my bag on the floor and sluggishly move to the lounge to flop down next to my dad.

"Petal," he smiles and leans into me, kissing me on the cheek.

"Hey daddy," I lean into him, and we sit like this as he watches the football highlights.

"How's the shop?"

"Busy," I sigh, "I feel exhausted. I need a holiday."

"Then book one," he says as if it is so simple.

"I can't do that, what about mum?" I frown.

"Your mum will be fine," he chuckles.

"What will I be fine with?" She asks as she places a glass of wine in my hand and a bottle of beer in my dad's. My eyes gaze at his bottle and my tummy flips. He clasps the same bottle that Crew drunk the other night.

Oh my god, get a fucking grip.

Why am I pining after him?

I take a large mouthful of wine and wince.

"Mum, this is disgusting."

She looks at me in shock then lets her eyes fall to the piss-coloured wine in her glass. "Well, I don't know why. It's chardonnay, cost me six quid."

"That's why," I heave. "Dad, can I have one of your beers?"

"Of course, my love."

I push off the sofa and dump the wine in the sink before grabbing a chilled beer from the fridge. Picking at the label for a moment I move down the hallway and find my phone, scrolling to his ridiculous nickname and typing out a message.

Dreamboat. Seriously?

I snort a laugh, bringing the bottle to my lips and take a mouthful as I watch the screen. Nothing. No double ticks. No turning blue. Disappointment soars through me but I shake it off and drop my phone back into my bag.

"So, did your team win?" I skip in and snuggle next to my dad.

"Of course, we did, buttercup."

DINNER WAS DELICIOUS AS ALWAYS AND I DECIDED TO walk home. The evenings were lighter, and the early summer air was beginning to warm, plus I liked the fresh air. It helped clear my foggy head. Pushing my earphones in I played *chaotic – Tate McRae* and it hit me in the feels.

I slow down as I turn the corner and I still. My skin smothering in goosebumps as the hairs on the back of my neck stand. I turn and see a white police car, an x5 to be precise. I cross my arms as he slows next to me, pulling into the kerb. The window slides down to show me his handsome face.

"Well hello, love bug."

I stick my finger down the back of my throat and gag.

"Veto?" His thick brows pinch.

"Yes! How you even have to ask that is beyond me." I scoff, shaking my head as my hair swooshes.

"Spoil sport." He winks.

"Busy?" Sarcasm is full in my voice.

"Extremely."

"I don't think your chief would be happy to know that a police officer of this community is following a citizen."

"I'm not following. You just happened to be where I was heading."

"Of course, *Dreamboat.*"

He laughs as he pulls to a stop outside my house. "Well, this is me, as you know." I narrow my eyes on him. "Stalker."

He holds his hands over his heart and acts wounded.

"Have you not got any noise complaints to attend to?"

"Not tonight, precious."

"Oh jesus, that's even worse than love bug."

He sighs and pulls a notepad out and scratches through two lines.

"What is that?" I shriek as I rush towards his open car window and my eyes bulge.

"My god," I laugh and take the pad from his hands. "Are these all the names you've come up with!?" I hold my stomach as I begin to laugh, hard.

"Well, one of them you'll like, surely."

"Hmm, going by that list you have no chance," I wink and step back.

"Do you want to get a drink? I am now…" he trails off and locks his eyes on his watch for a minute then smiles, "officially off the clock."

"I have an early start." I wince.

"Boooo," he sticks his thumb down, "poor excuse, come on, live a little," he wiggles his brow. I look at my own watch and smile. It's only eight.

"Fine, one. Two at the most…"

"Deal, I'll be back in half hour sweetie pie."

"Cross it off the bloody list!" I slap my hand to my head and groan before turning and climbing the steps to my front door.

Once the door is closed, I sink my teeth into my bottom lip and grin like the Cheshire cat.

Chapter Nine

Crew

I SIT AND WATCH HER ENTER HER HOUSE AND CLOSE the door; as soon as it's shut, I jive in my seat, cutting shapes with my hands that she said yes. I am in knots over this girl, and I have no idea why. I turn in the street and boot it back to the station, it's naughty of me to abuse my power but I don't want to make her wait, I reach up and flick the sirens on and weave quickly in and out of the traffic. Pulling into the carpark I rush from the car and launch the keys at Taylor behind the desk.

"You're in a hurry," she smirks as she hangs the keys up.

"You have no idea," I wink and push through the door to the changing rooms, ripping my body vest off and hanging it in my locker before tugging my top over my head. I don't fuck about; I pull my top on and replace my work trousers with my jeans. Pushing my feet into my trainers I run my fingers through my messy, brown hair. That'll have to do. Freshening up with deodorant then spritzing my cologne, I'm ready. I throw my hand up at Taylor as I rush to the carpark and jump in my *Audi RSQ8*. Pushing it into gear, I tear out of the carpark and head towards Cody. I have ten minutes.

I pull outside her house with two minutes to spare and I triumph in my small victory. I text back to the message she sent earlier, and it unsettles me instantly that I didn't reply.

> Sweet cheeks, I'm outside.

It turns blue as soon as it's sent, and she sends back vomit emojis.

> Another to scratch off the list.

I feel the magnet that is her, making me lift my head and my eyes pin to her, my jaw dropping. She has changed and now wears a black, ditsy daisy midlength dress. It's loose round her legs and arms but sticks to her curves as if it was made for her. She finishes off the look with *Doc Marten Sandals* and fuck she looks phenomenal. Rushing to push my door open, I stand on the pavement and reach out for her hand and spin her around just so I can let my eyes admire her for a moment longer.

"Hey," she blushes, her brown wavy hair falling forward as she drops her head.

"Hey," I walk her round to the passenger side, open the door and wait for her to climb in before strapping her in.

"I'm not a child," she frowns.

"I know you're not darling, but I want to make sure you're buckled in and safe," I reassure her, and I swear I see her heart thump through the bare skin showing on her chest.

I climb in my own side and start the engine, it roars, and she smiles, side eyeing me.

"Is this monster car to make up for your small willy?" She rolls her lips.

"How the fuck did you guess?" I act wounded as I drop my head, "Do you still wanna go out with me if I have a little worm pecker?"

"I would love to still go out with you, worm pecker and all."

I let out a throaty laugh before pulling into the road and heading towards our destination. How the fuck have I fallen for her this quick?

Sitting at the table, the server brings us over our drinks. Pornstar Martini for her, a beer for me.

She thanks and smiles at the waiter before her eyes land on mine and she smiles. I have never noticed just how blue her eyes were until now. I pick at the corner of the label that is plastered on my bud.

"You know, they say that means you're sexually frustrated." She brings the delicate glass to her lips and takes a mouthful, humming in appreciation.

"Does it now?" My brows lift as I continue to pick.

"Apparently... so, are you?"

"Sexually frustrated?"

She nods.

"Maybe," I shrug my shoulders up and take a mouthful.

"No Mrs in your life?"

"I hope not, seeing as I am here with you..."

"You can never be too sure these days," she lets out a heavy sigh.

"Lots of fake people," I nod.

"Dating apps don't work, yet I still go on them all."

"Why? You don't need dating apps," I scoff.

"Oh, I really do," she nods fast and drinks her whole drink down in one mouthful.

I sense this is not something she is comfortable with, yet I still push for more.

"Want to talk about it?"

"Honestly, there is nothing to talk about." Her head falls slightly, and I see her shoulders rise with the deep intake of breath that she takes.

"You ever been in a serious relationship?"

Her eyes meet mine in a steady gaze and she shakes her head softly from side to side and for some reason her answer fucking guts me. I didn't get it. She was fucking phenomenal. Yes, she was beautiful but in the short time I have known her there is more to her than just being stunning, beauty only runs skin deep but once you surpass that barrier there is so much more of her to get to know, I'm sure of it.

"How comes?" I want to stop asking but I can't. I need to get my head around this because nothing makes sense.

"Because I'm not girlfriend material, obviously," she scowls and catches the attention of the waiter. She orders another drink for herself.

"That's bullshit."

"It's really not," she scoffs, "I meet people on dating apps, we meet up and all they're interested in is sex. As soon as they've had their fun, they're hopping out the door quicker than a man running from a burning house."

"I don't believe you," I smirk but she doesn't return it, her eyes misty as they stay locked on mine and that's when I realise, she is telling me the truth.

"I can't even get a text back the next day, let alone them wanting to actually take me for dinner. I can't remember the last time I was taken on a date." She nods at the waiter as he places her cocktail in front of her.

"They're fucking idiots." I scoff, my brows pinching before they smooth out. "Why do you call them hoppys?"

"'Cause that's what they are. Hoppys. They hop in my bed then hop back out again," her cheeks blush, "you must think I am so easy, I'm not." She swallows down hard, her eyes falling to her fingers that are wrapped around the thin stem of her glass. I feel the deep ache in my gut.

"I didn't think that at all," I reach out, sliding my hand across the table to cover her small one with mine. "I'm just sorry you have never been loved."

She whips her hand from under mine and tucks a strand of her caramel brown hair behind her ear.

"It's just three words, they *mean* nothing."

I sit dumbfounded.

"Baby, if used in the right context, those three words *mean the fucking world.*"

She twists her pouty lips and sits back in her chair; I can see the glee spark across her baby blues.

The words fall on deaf ears, the silence surrounds us as I sit back in my own chair.

"I didn't mean for this night to take a nosedive," scrunching her nose she sloshes her drink in the bottom of her glass.

"Treacle, this evening hasn't nosedived," I smirk at her.

"Veto."

"Damn it!" I slam my hand down on the table.

She laughs loud and fuck, it's the most beautiful sound I have ever heard.

· · ·

PULLING KERBSIDE, SHE SLUMPS IN HER CHAIR AND exhales loudly. I tear my eyes from her house then face her. She smiles, and damn, it's the prettiest fucking smile.

"Thank you for tonight," her voice is soft as she tucks a strand of her hair behind her ear.

"What are you thanking me for?!" I smirk, "I should be thanking you for giving me a chance to take you out."

She scoffs, letting her head fall forward for a moment as she links her fingers together forming a knot.

"First date I have been on in a while," her head turns to face me, her eyes roaming over my face as if she is memorizing every feature.

"Well, if you are okay with it, I would like to ask you out again? Maybe a little more formal, you know, wine and dining..." I wiggle my brows trying to extinguish the tension that I can feel radiating from her.

"That would be lovely."

"Perfect."

I cut the engine and rush to her side to help her out of the car, but she is already out.

"Hey," I frown, "I am trying to be the perfect gentleman here," and she giggles.

"You already are the perfect gentleman."

I close the door behind her and link my hand through hers, her breath catching at the back of her throat from the contact.

"Is this okay?" I ask as we step onto the pavement, and she nods.

We walk to her door in silence, and I let go of her hand reluctantly. I gaze at her, trying to get my own emotions and feelings in check. This is the shit you read in romance novels, love at first sight and all that jazz. The fairy-tale feeling. That's what this was. I was living in a fairy-tale and I had no grip on reality. I hardly knew her, yet I feel like I have known her in every single lifetime. I feel like I am being pulled, the universe pushing us together as if we were each other's soulmates. But how is that possible? How is it possible to feel the way I feel about her. She is the breath I need to survive, the oxygen that fills my lungs every few seconds, the blood that swims through my veins and pumps into my heart. She is every beat.

And yet, standing here, taking in her radiant beauty all I want to do is say those three words that sit on the very tip of my tongue.

It would be so easy to let them spill out of me, for them three words to slice through me, ripping me open and letting my love for her bleed at her feet.

But I can't.

Because I don't know if she feels it too and it terrifies me.

"Do you wanna come in?" Her words pull at me, and I suck in a breath. *Yes, god yes.*

"As much as I want to, it's late. We both have work in the morning, but I'll see you soon okay?" I swallow the lump that has lodged in my throat, my stomach knotting at disappointing her.

"Oh, yeah, of course," she waves her hands in front of herself as if she *gets* it, as if it isn't a big deal when I know she is going to close that door behind her and let her mind run away with thoughts, overthinking every single move and thing she said tonight. She thinks I am going to be the new hoppy in her life.

"Does Friday work for dinner?" I ask, wanting to soothe the ache that is deep in my chest.

She nods, her eyes glassy. She turns her head quickly as

if not wanting me to see her but it's too late. Because I do. I always see her.

I hear the lock click, and she steps further away, and I feel the connection fading but the magnetic pull and urge I have to follow her overrides everything. I step forward, my foot on the edge of her threshold.

"Goodnight, Crew," she says quietly behind the door that she has shielded herself behind. Her cute, painted fingernails wrap round the edge of the door as she waits.

"Goodnight, Cody," I answer on a whisper and before I can retort back, the door is closed in my face, and I am left standing on the doorstep.

Shit.

———

Cody

Thursday came round quickly; I was anxious and I have no idea why. This wasn't a date, but what if sparks flew and it was one of those whirlwind love stories? I shake my head at my thoughts and continue to wipe down the sides. Crew invades my mind and guilt consumes me, making me feel sick to my stomach. He doesn't want you.

"You keep cleaning, we will have no counter tops left," Clarissa called as she walked past with a cup of tea and disappeared into the back office. Nervous laughter bubbled out of me as I dropped the cloth and antibacterial spray. She was right. Putting it away, I paced back and forth between the florist and the coffee shop. Pulling my phone out to check the time, he should be here any minute. I open the front camera of my phone and instantly regret it. I look fine, my hair is done, my make-up is done and there is no need for me to be this panicked.

Finding a spare table, I sit and people watch. Each time I see someone walking towards the shop from the distance, my heart flutters that little faster but they just carry on walking past. One of the girls runs me a coffee over and I thank her. Pulling my phone out, I notice he was twenty-five minutes late. He could just be running late? Maybe he missed his train? Or maybe he was just standing me up... I swallow down the bile that is creeping up my throat, rubbing my sweaty palms down the front of my jeans. It's fine, it's just a failed coffee date. It wasn't even a date! Exhaling a deep breath, my shaky hands reach for my coffee and I take a mouthful. This afternoon is just a reminder of why I don't date.

I was lost in my thoughts when an older gentleman sat at my table, his mature eyes glistening, a sweet smile pressed across his lips.

"Well, you're not who I was expecting," a small laugh escapes me as I stare at the man opposite me.

"Who were you expecting?" He asks, his frail, trembling hands wrapped round the top of his walking stick.

"A date... I think?" I shrug my shoulders up in a nonchalant way as I take a sip of my drink.

"Well, his loss is my gain. I'm Engelbert, Bertie for short," he holds his hand out and my smile only grows making my nose scrunch slightly and my eyes crease.

"Bertie," I repeat, "I'm Cody."

"So you think he stood you up?" Bertie scoffs a little while later as he places his cup of tea down on the saucer that came with it.

I nod, "Yup, it's the only explanation. I felt really bad for him, his wife cheated on him and his family told him to get back in the saddle," I sigh, tapping my nails on the side of my fresh cup of coffee. "But I am too kind hearted to see the best in people,"

"Did you believe him?" Bertie asks and I am shocked. "And that's not a bad trait to have."

"Of course, I did, if I didn't then I would be heartless and a monster," my eyes wide as I watch Bertie and he shrugs his shoulders up softly.

"You don't think he gave me a sob story just to..." I stop speaking suddenly. "Well... I never," I sit back in my chair, dumbfounded and shocked.

"Not saying it isn't a lie... but, who am I to know?" He smirks.

"I think I need to come off dating sites, but it's so hard to just go out and meet someone."

"Is it?" He asks.

"Seems that way, everyone I seem to meet either just wants..." I trail off and he nods, knowing exactly what I mean, "or they just want to be friends."

"Well, sometimes friendship leads to more..."

"And sometimes friends just stay friends."

"What will be will be," Bertie bows his head and I smile. He is right.

What will be will be.

Chapter Ten

Cody

"Do you need any help, Caroline?" I ask as I lean on the breakfast bar as she flaps around getting ready to serve dinner up. The weeks have passed in a blur. Bertie pops in once a week, as for Shane... I have no idea what happened to him.

"No, no love, I am okay. Just go relax." She looks over her shoulder at me and smiles.

But I can't just relax. I feel anxious and fidgety. Drumming my fingertips on the worktop, my eyes move from the side and down the hall where the front door is and back to Caroline.

After a moment, I hear the door catch go, I inhale, hold my breath and stare.

Our eyes catch each other's gaze, my heart flutters in my chest as he stands tall, a slow smile slipping on his lips.

We went from flirting, to stagnant, to friends to now... This.

Somewhere in between.

More friends than we are as anything else, but I am happy with that.

"Hey sugar lump," his voice echoes down the hallway and my heart thumps.

I stand and turn to face him as he strides towards me, all casual and shit. He is dressed in a round neck tee that clings to every part of his large, bulky frame. He wears black cargo trousers and a black cap covering his mop of messy, brown hair. We walk towards each other, each step getting faster until his arms are around my waist and mine are locked round his neck.

"Veto," I mutter against his tee, inhaling his musky scent.

I feel his body move as he laughs. Pulling away I turn to walk back towards his mum; his fingers wrap around my wrist and he tugs me back to him.

"You okay?" He asks softly, his eyes bouncing back and forth between mine.

"Yeah," I say a little chirpier than normal, "I'm fine. Why?"

"Just checking, that's all..." he trails off, lingering for a moment, his fingers press a little harder into my skin before he lets me go.

"Cool," I smile, continuing down the hall and back to his mother.

Dinner was delicious as always and Crew's mum and dad spent the evening, like they did every Thursday, telling me about him and his siblings as a child.

"Mum, pleaseeeee," he over exaggerated his plea, tipping his head back and rolling his head back. "Cody doesn't want to hear all of this."

I shuffle to the edge of my seat, placing my elbows on the table and smiling like a loon. "Uh, aha, I do." I nod.

"Elbows off," Caroline scolds me before turning her attention back to her son. I slip my elbows off the table and place my hands into my lap, twiddling with my fingers.

I met Caroline and Paul about two months ago, Crew kept begging for me to meet them and finally I gave in. Even though I haven't known them long, they're like my other parents. Crew also has three other siblings. Sailor, Scout and Wolf. I've met them once or twice and they're all as goofy as Crew.

I am bought back round to distant giggles and talking.

"Do you know how nice it is to have a girl in the family," Caroline smiles at me, reaches over and takes my hand.

"It's lovely to have you guys too," I blush because it's true.

"She's mine though mum," Crew pouts, leaning into me.

I roll my eyes.

"It's true," he nods towards Caroline and Paul.

"Oh stop it, don't be a possessive tool."

"Mum!" Crew snaps, his eyes narrowing on her.

"Well, nobody likes a possessive, dominating man, *Crew Mann.*" She leans on the table, her brows raising as her voice firms around his name.

"Maybe in the bedroom," Crew mutters under his breath and squeezes my thigh with his large hand and my skin burns. Then it hits me.

His fucking name.

"I'm sorry..." I stall, "your name..." I nibble my lip, stifling my laugh.

"What?" He looks at me then to his mum.

"Crew." I snort, "Crew Mann." Sinking my teeth deeper into my bottom lip, I can feel my cheeks ache as I try to suppress the smile that is begging to spread, my eyes glassy with unshed tears of laugher.

"See, mum, with the name..." Crew throws his head into his hand and screams.

"We think it's a good, fun name. Our little Crew Mann." His mum speaks in a baby voice, and I lose it. I lose all control, my eyes creasing as I burst into laughter, and I feel the hot tears rolling down my cheeks.

"Oh, petal, you haven't heard the worst of it," Crew groans.

"Stop it," I continue, and I see Paul's serious gaze and I know Crew is telling the truth.

"Please tell me."

"My brothers..." Crew looks at his mum who has a stupid grin on her face.

And then it hits me like a steam train.

Sailor Mann

Scout Mann

Wolf Mann

And I am dead.

CREW WALKS ME HOME; I ONLY LIVE A TEN-MINUTE walk from his parents. Crew lives about another fifteen minutes on, a little more in the city than me.

"Thanks for tonight, I had a good time," I smirk and kiss him on the cheek, "Crew Mann."

"Oh, piss off," he laughs, embracing me. "Lunch tomorrow? I feel like it's been forever, and from tomorrow night I am on shift for the next three days."

"I can't tomorrow, I am meeting Bertie at the shop," I smile softly, his eyes burn into mine.

"Cody," he holds his hand across his heart, "are you seeing another man behind my back?"

"Sorry, when did we become exclusive?" Smirking, I

feel my heart thump against my rib cage. One thing I have learnt with Crew is that he is a wind up, he loves to get a reaction from me.

"We haven't, I'm just stating how wounded I feel," he cups my face and I swear I feel my heart skip a beat, my skin burns from his touch. My breath catches as his lips hover over mine.

"Well, don't feel wounded," I manage to choke out, my eyes bouncing back and forth from his.

"Because we're just friends," he whispers, his eyes closing.

"Because we're just friends," the lump in my throat is large and wedged. I don't want to be just friends, but he has made no move to see what this is, or was between us. We work, and fuck I am adamant that we would be amazing together, but I am too hard. I'm not easy. I haven't had one hook up since meeting Crew because I don't want to. The thought of being with any other man other than him is too unbearable to even think about.

I step back, his eyes don't leave mine, but I need to put the distance between us because the pull to throw myself into him is too much, I can't handle it. Its unbearable, an uneasy weight that is slowly crushing my lungs minute by minute whilst I am this close to him.

"I hope your lunch with Bertie goes well," he gives me a crooked smile, his large hand rubbing round the back of his head.

"Thanks," I blush, "he is really sweet, he is a nice companion." The silence surrounds us for a moment. "When will I next see you?"

"Monday? Tuesday?" He fists one of his hands in the back pocket of his jeans.

"Monday is lasagne night," I shrug my shoulders up, "want to come?"

"Always, I'll meet you here and we can walk together?"

"Sounds perfect," nodding, I take a step up to the front door, Crew's hand finds mine as he tugs me back towards him. His lips part, his eyes falling to my mouth as he controls his breathing and I am silently begging for him to kiss me.

Minutes pass when he steps towards me and kisses my cheek, "Goodnight, Cody."

The disappointment surges through me and I push a fake smile on my face, nodding. "Goodnight."

I rush to push my key in my door and close it behind me. I can't bear to be close to him. I lock the door behind me and rush for my room, I need a cry, a soak in the bubble bath and bed. That's what I need. I am over emotional.

Chapter Eleven

CARRYING A COFFEE OVER TO BERTIE, I SMILE AS I SIT opposite him. This has become one of my favourite things to do. Once a week his daughter drops him off and we sit and talk for a few hours. His grey hair is always styled to the side, his bottle rimmed glasses take up most of his face. He always wears a suit and bowtie, and my heart explodes every damn time. After our first meeting, every week when we meet, he buys a single rose from my shop then brings it to the table with him to give me. He is such a sweet soul.

"How's your week been?" I ask as I pick my own coffee up and take a sip, it tastes good.

"Ah, you know," he waves his hand in front of himself, "same old for me, darling. I get up and get dressed. Read the paper over my cereal and then I sit and catch up with television until my daughter comes over and takes me out." He shrugs his shoulders up. "I sometimes wish she didn't because she has her own life, I don't need her rushing around after me and putting her own stuff on hold."

"But she wants to be there for you," I say softly.

"And for that, I will be forever grateful, but I can look after myself."

Oh, he is a stubborn man.

"Anyway, enough about me, what have you been up to?" He asks as his trembling hands reach for his cappuccino cup and I want to help him but no doubt he would smack my hand away.

I sigh heavily, sitting back in my seat wrapping my hands around the warm cup. My eyes move to the window as I watch the hustle and bustle of lunch time.

"What's there to say?" My eyes move back to Bertie. "I am too much of a wimp to tell Crew that I like him, and he is either the same or honestly just doesn't feel it." Bringing the rim of my cup to my lips I take a small mouthful, humming softly as I place it back on the table. I hear Bertie shuffle around in his seat as he places his elbows on the table.

"What I don't understand is why you wouldn't just tell him?"

"Because I don't want to be rejected." My cheeks blush.

"But you will never know unless you tell..." his bushy grey brow pops high onto his forehead.

"I know."

"You young kids confuse me," he chuckles as he sits back, reaching for his wooden walking stick and wrapping his fingers round the handle. I say nothing, I just nibble the inside of my lip.

"Back in my day, back when I met Dottie," his eyes fill slightly with unshed tears, "I was very persistent but respective," he smirks, I bet he wasn't. For some reason I feel like Bertie was a bit of a bad boy back in his day. "One day I decided to just go down to where she worked. She worked down at the Billingsgate fish market every Saturday morning, so I wanted to surprise her. I picked her fresh flowers from the little market stall near where I lived, her favourite were peonies," he pauses and smiles into the distance, as if reminiscing.

I just watch him, taking in this moment. He seemed to love her so much and I pray and hope that one day I get to experience a love like theirs.

"Sorry, lost my trail of thought for a moment," he chuckles softly, "but I marched down there, wearing one of my papa's old suits. It was far too big for me, but I made it work," he winks at me. "My thick brown hair was combed over. She was working with her father; I remember being so nervous." He wipes his cheek from a stray tear that had escaped, "but I puffed my chest out and looked her dead in the eye and asked her if she would like to go on a date, of course with her father's permission." He nodded, winking at me once more. "I gave her the flowers when she agreed, kissed her on the cheek which caused quite a stir and I ran as fast as I could before I was chopped and dissected like those fish that were laying in ice."

I laughed, my cheeks hurting from the smile that was plastered on my face.

"All went well on the date then?"

"Oh, very well. We began courting soon after that. You just need to be ballsy, what have you got to lose?" He asked as he shuffled in his seat again.

"Nothing."

"Exactly," he smiled, "worse case, he says no and you're just friends."

I sigh and it makes my heart ache at the thought of him saying no and rejecting me. I would much rather us stay friends then put any awkwardness on our relationship.

"Maybe I'll be a big brave girl soon, but at the moment, I am not quite ready to take that step."

He nods, "I get it, I do, but life is far too short..." he trails off, "don't wait forever, because you will always regret not telling him how you feel because it's gonna be like sucking eggs when he is with someone else. You'll always have the *'what ifs'*"

I swallow the lump down, forcing it back down before the hot tears begin rolling down my face. I know what Bertie is saying is true, but it still doesn't help me. I don't want to be the one to make the first move, but then if he feels the same as me both of us are going to be stuck in time.

The bell above the door dings and I turn to see Bertie's daughter Bailey walk towards us.

"Hey dad, Cody," she smiles and kisses her dad on the cheek.

"Hey," I wave, and Bertie goes all soft.

"Would you like a coffee?" I stand and offer her my seat.

"Yeah okay, that would be lovely."

"Not a problem. Bertie," I turn towards him, "would you like another one?"

"Why the hell not."

Smiling, I walk towards the kitchen area and get the coffee machine ready.

I make Bertie a bouquet of peonies like always to take to his wife's grave, it's become a little thing between us. He always tries to pay but I refuse.

"I'll see you next week?"

"Always," he bows his head and gives me a wink and I give him a massive smile.

. . .

CLEARING THE SHOP AWAY, MY MUM HAD THE NEXT two days off because next weekend we're at the races again. I sweep through and collect the last of the flowers that haven't sold today. Scooping them up and tying with twine then wrapping in brown parcel paper I place them on the counter. I remove my apron and hang it up on the back of the door to the back room. I hear the bell go on the door and inhale deeply.

"We're closed," I call out without turning round. There is no response, it gets my back up and I turn to see Crew standing there.

"Crew?" My eyes widen as he steps towards me, six foot of him wrapped in his uniform. My mind goes to places it shouldn't, his cuffs sit on his belt and all I can think about is him cuffing me to the bed. I shake my head.

"Is everything okay?" I was worrying, he was too quiet. He wasn't saying anything. He just walked towards me, his eyes pinned to mine, and I could feel the burn radiating through me, my skin tingling and the blood pumping quickly through my veins.

"I've been a fool."

"You have?" I ask as he closes the gap between us.

"I have," he nods.

"Why?" I whisper. Is this it? Is this where he is going to admit that he feels something for me?

"Because I haven't been honest with you, and I feel awful for it."

Thump, thump, thump.

"No?"

He shakes his head from side to side.

"Oh," is all I can manage, I swear this man steals my breath every. Single. Time.

His hand cups my face and I lean into it, my heart

warming from his touch. I never want to know what I would feel like without him.

Silence fills the room momentarily and his hand falls from my face. I want to whimper from the loss of his touch but I compose myself.

"I've got to move away for a while, it's been in the works for a couple of months. It's a massive step up from me just being on the beat all day, pulling drunk drivers over and turning up to noise complaints." His light blue eyes flit with glee at the memory of when he came to my house. But then the realisation of what he just says hits me like a freight train.

"What?" I whisper, stepping back until my back hits the wall behind me.

"I know, I have been wanting to tell you for weeks, but I don't know, I just thought that it may have not happened but now it has, I cannot not pass up this promotion..." his voice trails off for a moment. We both stare at each other, a thousand words waiting to be spilled out, but neither of us could fathom how to get the words out.

My heart pounded in my chest; how would I cope without him? He was such a big part of my life, my soul-mate and now he was leaving?

"When do you leave?" I manage to choke out, my lungs burning as I gasp in the air.

"Friday next week," he rolls his lips, fiddling with his radio that's clipped onto his vest.

"Right," I squeak out, fiddling with my fingers and knotting them together.

"Nothing is going to change, cookie."

"Veto," I grit out before a smile plays across my lips. I step towards him, "Everything is going to change."

"It's not."

"We will see, pumpkin."

"Pumpkin!?" He scrunches his nose up.

"Was just trying a nickname out on you," I wink.

Stepping towards me he wraps his arms around my waist and lifts me up.

"Well, *pumpkin*, I'll still be here."

"That's a lie, because you won't."

"No, Cody, I will still be *here*." His finger tracing an *x* over my heart.

"Okay..." I roll my eyes in an over-the-top kind of way, "cheese ball," and he smirks.

He presses his head against mine, no words are spoken, no words are needed.

This was our promise. He was still going to be with me. Wherever he was.

Chapter Twelve

WHY DOES IT FEEL LIKE MY HEART HAS BEEN RIPPED from my chest? It's not like he has died, he is just moving a few miles away. I lay with my eyes pinned to the ceiling as I let my thoughts bounce around my head until eventually, sleep wins.

When I wake my head is heavy and my body aches as if I have been ploughed by a steam train and I have no idea why.

First thing I do is check my phone, nothing. Dropping it into my duvet I lay for a moment longer. I need the girls. Pulling my sorry ass out of bed, I pad out to my kitchen and pop the kettle on. Coffee. Then girls.

"Hey," I say into the phone when I clicked Hallie's name. I always turn to Hallie first. Maybe because she knows me a little better, or maybe because she isn't as cutthroat as Mabel and honestly, my emotions are a little too high for her opinion at the minute.

"Hey, you okay?" She asks, I hear her closing and opening cupboards.

"Yeah, well, no, but yeah."

Silence.

"What one is it Cody? Yes or no?" I can hear a glint of humour in her tone.

"Both," I shrug my shoulders up as if she can see me. I tap my fingers on the side of my coffee cup.

"That bad huh?"

"I am being dramatic," I sigh.

"When aren't you dramatic?" She clicks her tongue against the roof of her mouth.

"Touché."

Silence.

"Babe, I love you. I do. But I am really busy and I haven't got time for you to sit here and play the silence game. What is wrong?"

"Crew."

"And what is wrong with Crew?"

"He is moving away."

"He is? Where to?" Her interest is piqued now.

"Few hours away."

"You'll still see him then."

"Only when he isn't busy, I know his shift pattern now. We have our days."

"Right?"

I sigh, my eyes falling to my lap as I nibble the inside of my mouth.

"Cody?"

"What if he meets someone? What if he falls head over heels in love and we never get the chance to explore what *this* is between us."

"You have no control over that, you can't stop him meeting someone darling. If it's meant to be it will be..."

"That's not what I want to hear," I snap and she laughs.

"What do you want me to say Cody? Go and move in

with him so you can keep him all to yourself? Because that's not fair on either of you. You can't force him to love you, yes I am being a bitch but you can't. You're friends. Neither of you were big enough to admit feelings."

"It just wasn't the right time," I mumble quietly and interrupt her.

"There is never a right time, Jesus Cody. Get out of your head, get out of the fairy-tale and stop moping. It's too late. You need to let him go." I hear the deep inhale that leaves her. "Sorry," she whispers, "I have a lot going on at home."

Blinking I let her words repeat.

"It's okay," I nod, what she is saying is right, but I still don't like it. But that's where the saying comes from. *Truth hurts.*

"Let him go Cody, if he comes back single then that's your time to tell him."

I hum in agreement.

"Is that you agreeing that you're going to let him go? 'Cause if not, I am going to come round and slap you."

Silence.

"What's the alternative, you do what I say and go and shack up with him?"

That's just it.

"And this is why I chose you to call. You always give the best advice." I beam, standing from the sofa.

"No, no, no Cody. That's not the advice I gave you."

"I'll call him and tell him. It'll be fine."

"Cody, sit your ass back on the sofa and do not, I repeat, *do not* follow Crew. Don't be that girl."

I stop in my tracks and let her words seep in.

"I wish I could, but I am just that. I am *that* girl." I thank her then cut the phone off, rushing for my bedroom.

I pace back and forth, watching my phone buzz on the coffee table in my living room. The girls have been blowing my phone up. First it was just Hallie, but then she got the other two involved and that is never good. Nibbling the skin on the side of my nail I stop for a moment and watch as my phone lights up constantly. I need to speak to Crew. I head towards the door of the flat, grab my keys and slam the door behind me, leaving my phone behind.

The whole walk to Crew's my stomach is knotting and my heart is slamming against my chest. The closer I get, the more I am regretting my choice. Is this a bad idea? Am I going to regret this and put me and Crew into an impossible situation? What if he doesn't want me to go? Oh god, I should turn back.

I still outside his house, knotting my fingers as I look up at the front door. Hesitating and fighting with my inner thoughts I take a step back and turn when I hear him.

"Cody?" He calls out and I freeze.

Fuck.

I turn slowly, holding my hand up.

"Hey."

"You okay?" His brows crease as he skips down the steps and stops in front of me, his eyes searching mine.

"Yeah fine," my tone blasé, my hand waving through the air. I step back.

"You sure?"

I nod.

"Then why are you here?" He tips his head to the side, his lips twisting as he tries to control his smirk.

"I was just in the area." *Jesus Christ, I am a shit liar.*

"Was you now?" He steps closer to me.

"Yup," I breathe out sharply. He scoffs a laugh then

fidgets on his feet, it's a hot minute before his eyes come to mine.

"I've been thinking..." He stills for a moment. His hand rubbing round the back of his head. This is nervous Crew.

"Yeah?"

He sighs, looking back at his house before looking at me again. The anticipation is killing me, my stomach is in knots.

"How easy would it be for you to give up work?"

My eyes widen.

Has he been wanting to do the same as me? Has he had the same thoughts?

"Honestly?" I lock my fingers together. "I would need to speak to my mum, it isn't just a job, is it? It's our business."

And suddenly, moving away with him doesn't feel like the right thing to do. My heart races, my throat is dry but I still try to swallow.

The silence radiates through us, both hearing the unspoken words. His breath is warm on my face, my skin erupting in goosebumps as his hand cups my cheek. The soft skin of his thumb rubbing across my cheekbone.

"Of course," his voice slices through the tension, "I get it, just ignore me. It was a stupid idea."

I nibble the inside of my lip before my eyes meet his.

"What was you going to ask me?" My voice is a whisper.

"I was going to ask you to come with me..."

I smirk, a small laugh sniffling out of me as tears begin to fill my eyes.

"Sunflower, what's wrong?" Now both of his hands are cocooning my face, holding tight but not in a vicious way. His big blue eyes bounce back and forth between my ice blues.

A stray tear rolls down my cheek and I feel my heart

constrict against my rib cage. "I was coming to ask you the same thing," I whisper as another tear falls.

His hands drop from my face, and he falters back a step, his eyes widening as the realisation hits him.

We were both feeling and thinking the same.

Chapter Thirteen

Crew

RUNNING MY HAND ROUND THE BACK OF MY HEAD, I AM lost for words. I am normally no good in these *reading people* situations, but now I feel like I am certain that she feels the same for me. That she wants to be more than friends?

Her big blue eyes are willing for me to talk, to say something, but I am afraid to say the wrong thing.

She knots her fingers, linking and pulling on them as her eyes pin to mine.

"You wanted to come with me, like... as in..."

Her eyes widen and she drops her hands.

"Friends."

"Of course, friends," I laugh nervously. *Fuck it. Maybe I can't read people like I first thought.*

"Of course," she waves her hand through the air, "look, I better get going... lunch tomorrow?"

"Yeah, yeah, lunch sounds good. I am on shift but I'll come around one before I start at three," I nod softly.

"Perfect, see you then?"

"See you then, cookie crumb," I call out as she begins to walk away.

"VETO!"

I smirk and wait for her to disappear before I head back inside. My heart aches, rubbing my chest to try and soothe it. How could I have got it so wrong? I don't get it. Pulling my phone out my pocket I click on my messages and find the group with the boys in. I need them.

> Lads, meet me in the bar at four?
> Emergency.

WILL

> Make it five and I can be there.

HARRY

> Five is perfect.

RICHARD

> Oh dear, has it finally happened? Have you grown a pussy and become BFFs with Cody?

> Fuck off. See you at five.

Rolling my eyes, I throw my phone on the floating shelf underneath the black framed mirror. I feel myself getting wound up, it's not like I can just call her up and come out with it. She's made it very obvious that she just wants to be friends, and now it's time that I let her go, time for me to move on. I've been pining after her for nearly four months and there isn't an ounce of mutual feelings back from her. She wants to be just friends, then that is what she is going to get.

. . .

I sit in the bar with my friends, the waitress placing our beers down in front of us. I smile at her, she's cute. Bobbed red hair and deep green eyes.

"Thanks," I continue to stare, and she dips her head, smirking before she walks away. I jump up and grab her wrist.

"Do you want to get a drink sometime?" I shoot out and her eyes dance with mine, I see the glee shoot through them.

"Sure, yes. That would be lovely," she fiddles in her waitress apron and pulls out her notebook, jotting her number down then passing it to me.

"Thank you..." I pull my eyes from her and look at her name, "Candy." She blushes.

"I'm Crew."

"Nice to meet you Crew."

"I'll call you," I fold the paper and slip it into the back pocket of my jeans.

"I'll look forward to it," her voice is sweet and quiet before she turns and heads into the back.

Puffing my chest out, I take my seat back next to Will.

"Why did you do that?" He asks a little stunned.

"Because I need to move on from Cody, it's obviously never going to happen."

He scoffs. "You don't know that."

"No, I don't, but I think she has made it pretty fucking clear." I drink down my beer and slam the empty glass on the table.

Their eyes widen as they watch me.

"Well, doesn't little Cody get under your skin," Harry sits back in his seat and crosses his arms across his chest.

"Wait, aren't you meant to be at work?" Richard asks.

"Called in sick," I scowl as I look at my empty glass,

"I'm debating this whole move to be honest, I just don't know what to do anymore."

"You're a fucking idiot if you give up that promotion," Harry glares.

"Then maybe I am a fucking idiot." I sigh, "I feel like I have been gutted, like, I feel physically sick at the thought of leaving her." Rolling my lips I let my eyes stay on my glass, "How pathetic is that?"

"Pretty pathetic mate." Harry shakes his head from side to side softly.

"You can't give up on her," Will pipes up from beside me.

"Seems like he already has," Rich smirks, "he has the hot little waitress' number already."

Will groans as he sips his beer, "I just think you're giving in a little too easy Crew."

"I'm tired of thinking one thing but her showing me something different. It's for the best, we can both just meet other people and crack on with that. As for me and her, we can just stay friends."

They stay silent.

"You do choose them don't you," Harry smirks.

"I do," I sigh, "anyway, dickheads, tell me... what's new with you lot?"

By the time we leave the bar I am ridiculously tipsy and can't see straight, not a good move. I stumble out the taxi and wave to the guys before trawling up the steps to my front door. It takes me a hot minute to slip my key into the lock before I tumble through.

"Jesus Christ," I groan, rubbing my elbow that I smashed on the doorframe. Chucking my keys on the shelf I pad through the short hallway and into the kitchen, just to the left of me. I live in a small mid terraced Victorian house. I loved all the original features like the tiled mosaic floor that leads through the entire downstairs. The kitchen is a small rectangular room, the kitchen cabinets a grey shaker with a marble worktop. I gave this room a little make over when I moved in. The lounge still has the old ornate fireplace which is the focal point of the room, the room is white with black, high back leather sofas. Again, low maintenance. My house is tidy, but it's easy to keep a little two up two down clean when it is just you. Slamming the fridge door shut after grabbing a bottle of water, I drag my tired feet up the stairs. Stripping off, I climb under my sheets naked, and my mind fills with Cody.

Instantly my dick is hard and in my hand. I imagine what her sweet little cunt would feel like around me, how she would taste on my tongue and feel on my fingers. My fingers tighten around myself as I pump my hand up and down slowly. I can already feel my balls begin to constrict, the feeling of my impending orgasm smothering my skin in goosebumps. I groan, tipping my head back and letting my cum spurt out all over my stomach and hands. Curling my neck up, I look at the mess then fall back down again.

I need to get a grip.

Slipping back under my sheets after a quick, cool shower, I feel a little more relaxed and surprisingly not as tipsy.

I open my messages and find her name, my thumb hovering over it for a bit before I lock my phone. Nothing good will come from it so best to leave it before I open a huge can of worms. It's already complicated, I don't want to make it worse. I roll my lips, I'm seeing her for lunch tomorrow, I can talk to her then. I lean up and place my phone down on the bedside table and then roll onto my back willing for sleep to claim me. Willing my mind to be consumed with anything other than Cody.

Laying with my thoughts for a while longer, I make the conscious decision to sleep on my job offer. Do I really want to give it all up for Cody?

Chapter Fourteen

Cody

THE MORNING AT WORK WHIZZES BY, AND I AM grateful because I am dead on my feet. Sleep didn't come easy to me last night because I was replaying what happened with Crew repeatedly. I should have said more, I should have admitted to him and not lied about why I was outside his house. *Such an idiot* my subconscious reminds me.

I look at the time and my heart begins to drum faster, he should be here soon. I busy myself behind the counter, checking through the order book when I hear the bell above the door ding. My eyes lift and I see him walking towards me. My heart swells in my chest and I clench myself to ease the ache that comes whenever I see him.

"There's my girl," he smiles, leaning over the counter and giving me a kiss on the cheek. I blush as he pulls away and move round the counter to be near him.

"How's your day been?" I ask as I lead us through to the little coffee area and take a seat in the empty window seat. Mum bounds over as soon as our bums are on the chair and Crew is back up and cuddling her as they talk and I just watch and listen. Him and my mum have a lovely relationship and I am grateful that they get along.

She disappears and Crew sits back down and wiggles his eyebrows.

"Your mum so wants me."

"Stop it you twat," I giggle and swat him with the menu.

"Only joking," he winks before his smile slips and his eyes burn into my skin, "you look tired, you okay?" He shuffles in his seat and thanks my mum as she places a cup of coffee in front of both of us.

I nod, picking my cup up and letting my fingers wrap around the china to keep them busy. My mum darts off to the kitchen before I speak.

"I didn't sleep very well last night," I admit as I blow on my oat latte.

"Neither did I," he licks his lips of the froth from his cappuccino as he places the large cup back on its saucer.

"No?" My voice creeps up an octave or two and he shakes his head. "Look I'm sorry about last night, I—"

"Don't apologise, honestly," he holds his hands up and smiles at me, "you have nothing to be sorry for."

I shrug, "Well, I kind of do, you see..." I stop as he looks down at his watch that is vibrating on his wrist, then he slips his phone out and clicks the ringer off.

"Sorry."

"It's fine," picking under my nail I open my mouth and continue.

"I've got something to tell you," he mumbles but I miss it because I am too focused on getting the verbal diarrhoea out.

"I wanted to come with you so we could live together and see what this is between us," my index finger moves back and forth between us.

"I've met someone," he finishes at the same time and our eyes lock, my own widening as the sinking feeling anchors me when I realised what was said between us.

"Candy," his voice is soft, and I scrunch my nose up.

"Ew, Veto."

"No, no, shortcake," he nervously laughs. "That's her name. Candy."

"Here we go darlings, two ceaser salads," my mum's voice crashes through us as she places our lunches down. I can feel her eyes penetrating mine, but I cannot fathom how to turn to look at her. It's as if I was paralysed, frozen and anchored to this very spot.

He's dating!?

I hear my mum's footsteps retort back to where she came from but my eyes are still on Crew.

"You're dating?" I choke out.

"You wanted to come with me!?" His voice is louder as he pushes his hand through his thick, soft brown hair in frustration.

"And you're dating?" I ask again.

"Not dating as you think, I asked for someone's number."

I feel like I could throw up. I swallow down and reach for my glass of water and try to swallow down the lump in my throat. By his reaction he either didn't hear everything I said, or he is choosing to ignore it so it's not awkward that I basically admitted to wanting more while he told me he wants to date another woman. Why is this bothering me? Why am I so worked up over this? We're friends, we have never said we are more than that, so why is it leaving such a bitter, sour taste in my mouth.

I nod subconsciously along to whatever he is saying while feeling completely numb inside.

"Cody," he says louder and pulls me out of my thoughts.

"Yeah?"

"Are you okay?" I can hear the sincerity in his voice, my face falls slightly.

"I think so," shrugging my shoulders up and reaching for my coffee cup, spinning it on the table.

Silence falls and I realise it's time to push my jealousy down. Time to pull my big girl knickers up.

"So, tell me all about Candy," I breathe out and smile and the corners of his mouth lift. I need to be his friend. That's what we are.

Friends.

The pain that seared through my gut made my breath catch but I played it down.

Crew shuffles in his seat as he begins to tell me what his plans were with Candy.

It's all going to be fine.

Fine.

Chapter Fifteen

Cody

I SAT IN MY KITCHEN WAITING FOR THE GIRLS TO COME over, my fingers drumming on the worktop as I gaze at the two bottles of wine, the condensation from the fridge running down the sides. Me and Crew haven't spoken about our lunch all those months ago since that day, like a silent agreement to bury it deep and never let it resurface. I told myself that things had gone on for too long, we were both too stubborn to say anything and I was too late, but that doesn't mean that I don't think about him every single day. He is my first thought of a morning and my last thought before I close my eyes. The ache in my chest pulls and reminds me that my heart is still not okay with this arrangement, but it has to be. Crew's heart doesn't belong to me.

His heart belongs to Candy.

I gag. At the beginning I had hoped that he and Candy wouldn't work out, what with him planning to leave so soon after, but fate was not on my side. Crew's move was delayed for a few months, meaning they were able to date properly.

I'm startled out of my thoughts when I hear a knock on my door. Thank Christ. Rushing up, I run down the hall and swing the door open. Mabel, Tia and Hallie are standing with snacks.

"Beauts," my shoulders fall forward as I instantly relax.

"Hey, hey," Mabel chimes as she brushes her shoulders with mine as she waltzes in smelling like roses and dressed in an expensive silk blouse and high waisted pencil skirt. I'm not sure why she is so dressed up for takeaway and wine? Did I miss the memo? And then I see Tia and Hallie looking as scruffy as me and sigh in relief. Closing the door behind Hallie, I grab her elbow and pull her back towards me.

"Why is she dressed up to the nines?" I whisper.

"I asked her the same, apparently she hasn't been out in so long that she felt the need to dress up," she shrugs her shoulders up before she stands next to me, both of our eyes fixated on her. She seems so carefree when she is without the baby, not that I know what it is like.

"Fair enough," I mutter and step into the open planned lounge and kitchen area. Mable is already pouring the wine out into the glasses and Tia is on her phone looking at take-aways. She looks like she is ready to drop, her bump is popping out a lot more now. She is due near Christmas so not long left at all. Excitement bubbles inside of me at the thought of a brand-new baby.

"So, I've been thinking..." Hallie says as she slides my wine glass across the marble breakfast bar to me.

"Mm," I hum as I take a mouthful. That first sip always hits different. Especially on a Friday.

"Can we arrange a night out with Crew and his lot?" Her words are rushed as she takes a large mouthful of her wine, her eyes pinned to me before they slowly round the other two girls.

"I could?" I mumble and the anxiety crashes through

me at the thought of going out with Crew and possibly Candy.

"I just think we had so much fun with them all that time ago and his friends are such a good laugh, and you know, it would be nice to see Will again." Her cheeks blush a crimson red and I get it. They had a connection when we last went out.

"Oh yay, that'll be so much fun," Mabel claps excitedly.

"I'll message him," I nod, but my stomach is in knots at having to contact him. It's not that we haven't spoken to each other or seen each other but going out, drinking and being in close proximity is dangerous. For my sanity that is.

"Thank you," she chimes.

"Everyone good with Italian? I am craving a carbonara."

"Sounds good," we all agree and Tia places the order.

MABEL AND TIA ARE SITTING ON THE SOFA CHATTING away and me and Hallie are in the kitchen cleaning up after dinner.

"How are things with you and Derek?" I ask blasé as if it's the normal conversation for us.

"Meh," she shrugs her shoulders up quickly, "things aren't great, I just don't know if I have much more fight left in me. It's been a long fifteen years," she sighs and places her bubble covered hands on the edge of the chrome sink. My heart constricts in my chest.

"Hal," I breathe, my voice a whisper so the others don't hear. Not that they would judge, well, I don't think they would, but Mabel would be the one to put her two pence in if anyone.

"It's fine, we're both in agreement. We're going to break

it off and stay amicable. It's not like we have children to consider in this decision."

"Are you okay?" I finally manage to ask, because my heart is breaking for her.

"I will be," she turns to face me, her eyes are glassy but her smile is wide.

"What are you doing about the house?"

"Splitting everything fifty-fifty. Fair then, isn't it?"

I nod.

I pull my marigolds off and hang them over the side of the sink, letting them drip as Hallie dries her hands on the hand towel.

"So, this is why you want to go out with Crew? Well, Crew and his gang."

She nods, "Well more so to see Will." There's that blush again.

"You like him huh?"

She nods again, "We've been speaking, we're friends. I confide in him with my issues and vice versa," her smile slips, "I'm worried he will stay with Lucia."

"His wife?"

"Mmhmm."

"What has he said?"

She stalls, looks over her shoulder and smiles at Mabel and Tia chatting away, completely oblivious to us standing here.

"That he is walking away from her, but he has his son. It's not as easy for him as it is for me." A heavy sigh leaves her.

"Have you... you know?" Her eyes widen, gasping.

"God, no. No, no. Purely just friendly. We haven't even exchanged flirty or dirty texts." She shakes her head from side to side. "I couldn't do that to Derek, I'm not a cheater. I still care a lot for him, I love him but I'm not *in* love with him."

"I know you're not," I smile and hook my arm around her shoulder, pulling her into me and kissing the side of her head.

"I am proud of you for taking this next step, it's a big change."

"It is, isn't it." Her lips curl at the corner.

"It is," I nod.

"Wine?" She asks as she breaks away from me and opens the fridge and I smile.

MABEL FLICKS GOSSIP GIRL ON AND WE SIT QUIETLY for a moment as we watch the love story that is Chuck and Blair. I look at my phone, I still haven't plucked up the courage to text Crew.

"Have you heard back from him?" Hallie says quietly, leaning into me.

"I haven't text him yet..." I touch the screen on my phone, waking it up again.

"Oh."

I feel bad suddenly, so I find his name and begin to tap, all the time my heart racing in my chest.

> Hey, how are you? When are you and the guys free? The girls want a night out xx

Swallowing down the nerves, I press send and wait.

And wait.

Getting annoyed, I exit out the message and turn my phone upside down.

"I've text him; he is probably with Candy so won't reply straight away." I try to say with no emotion in my voice. I feel like I am ready to break, and once I crack, I won't be able to put myself back together again.

"Eugh, Candy." Tia tsks and I hear Mabel groan.

"Look, he is happy. I was too immature to pull my finger out and do something about it so now I have to sit and watch him fall in love with someone else," a sad smile tries to lift the corners of my mouth, but it doesn't quite make it. "Plus, he is leaving soon anyway so hopefully he leaves Candy behind."

I see Hallie's eyes bat back and forth from mine, her lips are twisting as she rubs her palms up and down her jean covered thighs.

"Hallie," I bolt forward, my eyes pinned to hers now. *She knows something.*

"What?" She plays dumb and I narrow my gaze.

"What do you know?" Mabel jibes at her.

"Nothing..." she rolls her lips and looks at her freshly manicured nails.

"Hallie," my tone is sterner now, I can feel my chest constricting as my heart thrashes around in my chest.

"Will told me in confidence," she blurts out and her eyes widen to what has just left her lips.

"Told you what?" Mabel swipes in, completely ignoring the name that slipped out.

She huffs and sighs before fiddling with the skin around her nails.

"Hallie," Tia moans.

"Fine! Candy is going with him," she blurts out before slapping her hand over her lips and her eyes bugging out of her head.

And I swear my fucking heart falls from my chest. I'm still trying to find the words but at the moment I am sitting, mouth agape and my eyes wide as I just stare at Hallie. I am so lost in thought that I don't even hear my phone beep. Mabel throws it on my lap, and I tip my head forward and see Crew's name flashing on my phone with an unread message. I smirk at the emojis at the end of his name, a crown and a unicorn. My thumb brushes across the screen of my phone, I always thought he was going to be my king, riding in on a magical unicorn and saving me. Whisking me away and riding us into our happily ever after.

But now, he was going to be riding into the sunset with fucking Candy.

"Are you okay?" Mabel asks, wrapping her arms around me.

"I'm fine," I laugh, running my index finger under my eye to stop the stray tear that tried to escape. "We have never been more than friends."

It was the truth.

We never have, we never will. Swallowing down, I shrug my woes off and open my phone as I wait for the message to load.

CREW

Hey poppet, I was just talking to the guys about a leaving do – how does next Friday work? Can't wait to see you. I miss your face. I've been waiting for your photo to pop up on the milk cartons because you seem to be missing from my life...

I scoff.

Friday is perfect. Well, you're a taken man now so I thought I better take a step back. You know how girls get when they find out their boyfriends have girl best friends.

I try to lighten the mood but it's the truth. Girls hate

their boyfriends with girl mates. It's a fact and anyone who says they're okay with it is a big fat liar.

"Next Friday good for you all?" I look up from my phone, ignoring the beep that just vibrated in my lap.

"Perfect," they all say apart from Tia.

"I'll give it a miss, I'm too pregnant to go out." She huffs, rubbing her belly with tenderness.

"George is out scouting but mum will have baby for me."

"So, we're going then?" I try to sound happy, but I am full of dread. Jesus, when did I become so damn needy and miserable? I need to suck it up. There is more to my life then fucking Crew.

Damn, I didn't even get to fuck him. What a waste.

Shaking my head, I pull myself together.

"Yup, only if that's okay with you?" Hallie says, her tone flat but her smile is saying something completely different. She's excited. I get it. I would be too if Candy wasn't going to be there. Flipping my phone over, I open his message.

CREW

Candy knows the deal. You were my friend first. You'll always be my friend first x

And there's that knife being plunged into my heart and twisted round until I can't physically bleed anymore. The air is knocked from my lungs and suddenly I am gasping for breath. I rush to the window, lifting the handle up and pushing the window as wide as it would go to let the crisp autumn air fill my lungs. I know the girls want to know what's wrong, well, they know what's wrong. They want to know the reason I am acting like this, I *want* to know why I am acting like this. I need a date. I need sex. I just need to get under someone to get over Crew and as much as my meetings with Bertie are lovely and sweet, it's not helping with my schoolgirl crush. Closing my eyes, I inhale deeply, sucking cool air in. I can do this. I am pining over someone who has moved on. I need a hoppy.

I spin, push my chest out and let my shoulders fall back. The girls' eyes are on me and I see a hint of a smile on Mabel's lips.

"Girls, I need your help."

Chapter Sixteen

Cody

STANDING IN FRONT OF THE FULL-LENGTH MIRROR I twisted round then looked over my shoulder at my behind. I smirk. Spinning back round, I looked myself up and down, tilting my head to the side. I was wearing a black and cream geo skort and a black body suit. My brown hair was straight and my new bangs I had cut in was styled in a blunt straight. My ice blue eyes were surrounded by a smudged, black eyeshadow and finished with a pop of eyeliner. I loved how my eyes stood against the darkness, a nice contrast. I finished the look with my beige *Alexander McQueens*. I couldn't afford them, but they had my name all over them, to be honest, the store assistant saw me coming from a mile off with my soppy, sad look and said the way to get over heartbreak was a new pair of shoes. So now I have six hundred pounds added to my credit card balance for a pair of trainers that make me feel like I am part of the *Spice Girls*.

Grabbing my small Mulberry cross body bag, I loop it over my shoulder, so it sits just above my hip. I feel nervous but excited. This is the first date I have been on since

Crew. *There's that ache again.* Rubbing my chest to ease it, I spray my floral perfume and check my phone to see if Julian has cancelled. He hasn't. We arranged to meet at *Devonshire Terrace* at Liverpool Street. I can hop on a train and be there in under half an hour. He wasn't my usual type, but sometimes opposites attract and all that. He is tall, really tall. Unlike Crew who is just under six foot. Julian has dirty blonde hair that is long on top and perfectly styled. Crew has the most beautiful chocolate brown hair that always looks a mess whether he does it or not. Julian is toned and sculpted and looks like a son of *Zeus* or *Thor.* Where Crew is solid, broad and is a *big* boy in all ways. He is the definition of Dad bod and I am here for it. I would much rather Crew than Julian, but Crew doesn't want me. The sooner I get that through my thick head the better.

Letting out a deep sigh, I move forward and walk towards the front door, grabbing my keys off the side table and stepping outside into the cool evening air. I shrug my three-quarter length armed blazer on and lock the door behind me. Popping my earphones in, I press play on *Dress – Taylor Swift* and all I can think about is Crew. Skipping the song *Thrice – Artist in the ambulance* begins playing and I smile. This is better.

Stepping out at Liverpool Street I make my way down the side roads and towards my destination. Nerves begin to grip me, knotting my belly as I get closer with each step I take. He has been really sweet, sure we have only been speaking for a few days but he makes me laugh and smile and seems like he will treat me like a princess.

Walking into the open roof terrace, I frown slightly at the fake flowers that wrap around the bars and hang over the main entrance. This placed would be lovely in the summer and I sigh. Moving sheepishly towards the steps to the waitress stand where she is waiting.

"Hi, table for one or are you meeting someone?" She asks, smiling as she slips two menus into her hands.

"Meeting someone," I say a little breathless as my eyes gaze behind her and that's when I see him. Crew with Candy.

"Fuck," I mutter and dip my head, moving to the side in case Crew sees me.

"Everything okay ma'am?"

"Yup, fine." I whisper shout, fumbling in my bag, I find my phone and hold up Julian's photo. "This is who I'm meeting."

She smiles, "Ah yes, he is just through here in the back terrace."

Thank God.

Slipping in the door, I give one last glance at Crew and Candy, and I smile. Genuinely smile. He is happy. He deserves to be happy.

And so do I.

We both do.

Nerves take over but I smile when I see Julian sitting there, his eyes alight with glee and his smile continues to spread across his lips, then his green eyes rake up and down my body. He stands from his chair and rushes towards me as he takes my hand in his and rubs his thumbs across my knuckles and my skin tingles, but not in the way it normally does when it's Crew. I smile nervously before he moves behind me and pulls my chair out. I take my seat and thank him before he joins me. He is handsome, pretty even. Long black lashes that fan on his face, his skin a beautiful glow to it and a dusting of freckles across his nose and cheeks.

"Can we start with drinks?" The waitress asks, her eyes pinned to Julian's.

"I'll have a gin and tonic please," he nods before his face turns towards me.

"I'll have an espresso martini please," I beam as I knot my fingers in front of me on the table. I planned with Hallie that I'll text her in an hour if it's not going well, then she will call with an emergency. If that backfires, she knows someone who works here who will help me.

"It's nice to meet you..." he trails off, "face to face," he smirks leaning his hand across and placing it over my trembling one.

"You too," a laugh bubbles out of me, "sorry, I'm nervous. I haven't been on a date in a while," I quickly slip my hand from underneath his and reach for the jug of water that is sitting in the middle of the table. Pouring my glass full, I drink the whole thing. I am parched. Or is it just the nerves?

Julian sits back in his chair and runs his finger across his plump bottom lip and my eyes widen. *Is he trying to flirt?*

I breathe a breath of relief when the waitress places our drinks down. We fall into easy conversation about our jobs, schools and plans for the future. Julian owns his own fit out company, small scale he says but I'm not sure if he is playing it down. He has fitted a few of the big-name shops, apparently. You can't take everything as gospel when you're in the early stages of dating. He could be spinning me a web of lies or living a second life. He knew where my flower shop was and said he had passed it a few times when out and about, but truthfully, it's hard to miss. Flowers outside and climbing one side of the shop and a beautiful deep, green wooden door.

"I am thinking of expanding through to the empty shop next door." I say through a mouthful of fish.

"Oh really?" His brow lifts and he takes a sip of his gin. I am trying my hardest to not think about Crew out there, but yet he still manages to fill my mind.

"Yup, the shop next door is due for lease in the next few months and I would love to expand my little corner library and have it as a book store where people can get their coffees or whatever and just let the day slip away while lost in a good book," I sigh happily and I realise this is the first time I have told anyone but my mum about my plans.

"That sounds amazing Cody, well, I would always be happy to come and have a look once you get the lease."

"*If* I get the lease."

"You'll get it," he winks before holding his hand up to the waitress to order another round of drinks, my cheeks pinching with a red tint.

We're on our third round of drinks when I feel my skin prickle, the hairs on the back of my neck stand and I know he is here. I rub my hand round the back of my neck and dip my head because I don't want him to see me.

"You okay?"

I nod, not wanting to speak. I see Julian look around the restaurant then back at me.

"Cody?" His voice vibrates through to my core and I'm putty in his hands. I melt. Literally. I plaster a smile on my face and spin to face him and *her*.

"Oh my god," I act surprised, "Crew?! Fancy seeing you here," I laugh, standing and wrapping my arms round his neck to hug him. I feel her eyes burning into the back of my head and I feel my throat tighten, my chest constricting at being in his arms and our hearts beating steadily together. Like our hearts were made to sing in harmony.

I feel his large, thick arms tighten round my waist and he inhales deeply as his nose is buried in the crook of my neck.

I pull away because this looks suss.

"How rude of me, sorry," I tuck a loose strand of hair behind my ears and step away from my best friend. "Crew, this is Julian, my..." I stall, my thoughts being snatched from me and suddenly, I feel like I have lost the ability to talk.

"Her boyfriend," he finishes the sentence for me as he stands and shakes Crew's hand with a tight grip and I just stand there like a fucking idiot.

"Boyfriend?" And that's when I see it. The cockiness in Crew's voice and the flash of jealousy firing in his bright blue eyes and I can't help but smirk.

"Yup," I play along, standing next to Julian as he wraps his arm around my waist and pulls me further into him. Crew's jaw clenches and he scoffs, running his hand round the back of his neck then messes his already tousled hair and I can't work out if it's a flare of anger or regret that is rearing its ugly head deep inside his belly.

Candy coughs softly and all eyes move to the petite and pretty redhead, and it annoys me that she is so beautiful. I lift my chin and smile as if it she isn't gnawing at my insides.

"Cody, and..."

"Julian," I pipe up, my voice a little higher pitched as I answer, and I am fighting my smile. Julian's fingers dig into my hip.

"Julian," he grunts out, "this is Candy, my..."

"Girlfriend, I'm his girlfriend. It's going really well," her speech is fast as she holds her hands out for us to shake and we do, even though touching her feels wrong. I don't like the feeling I get off her, but then again, I'm bitter so I would feel that way.

"We've been speaking about taking our relationship to the next level, haven't we fuzzy butt?"

My eyes widen and I bite my lip to stop my laugh. *Fuzzy Butt. Fuck I am dead.*

"Yes," his eyes don't leave mine and I can see the pain in them.

Silence slices through us, the tension thick and the air crackling between me and Crew. It's unbearable and suddenly, I can't breathe.

I choke, stepping back before I cough and splutter.

"Excuse me, one moment," I smile at Julian and walk with my head down towards the bathroom. Barging through the doors, I cling my fingers round the edge of the sink and close my eyes, inhaling a deep breath to try and fill my lungs with the breath that he snatched. Slowly my eyes lift, and I stare at myself to see a quote written in chalk on the mirror.

STOLEN GLANCES, WANTED KISSES, TWO LONELY BEATING *hearts.*

I SHAKE MY HEAD FROM SIDE TO SIDE AND STAND TALL, staring back at the girl who is looking back at me. *What are you doing?* I lick my lips and taste saltiness from a tear that has run down my cheek. I swipe it away when I hear the bathroom door slam and I see Crew.

Eyes narrowed on me, jaw clenched and chest heaving.

"Crew?" I step back from the sink and my eyes take his persona in. I see a hint of a smile that doesn't fully meet his beautiful eyes like it usually does. Icy blue eyes glazed as they fall to my heaving chest.

My voice snaps him from his zombie stance, blinking

when his eyes meet mine and I feel home. The thump in my chest reminding me not to forget Julian is out there.

He steps forward, his shoulders dropping as they relax. His large, callous hand cups my cheek and I automatically lean into it.

"I was just coming to see if you were okay, pudding."

"Veto," I breathe through a laugh. "How are you doing *fuzzy butt*," I taunt, stepping away and breaking from his captivating trance that I seem to fall under when he is near.

"Hey, leave my fuzzy butt out of this." He smirks and fists his hand into his pockets.

"Seriously though, is she a cheese ball like you?"

"Nah, she just has these weird, cute ass names. I don't like it but yano, we roll with it." He rocks on his toes before pushing back onto flat feet. "So, Julian seems *nice*." I can hear the sarcasm in his voice, but I choose to ignore it.

"He is," I nod, looking past him at the door, "same as Candy," I smile.

"She is," he nods, firm.

And for the first time in a long time, awkward silence consumes us.

"You know I'm always here for you right?" He rubs his hand over his hair.

"Of course, right back at you," I wink.

I take that as my cue to leave, I step towards him and move towards the door when he steps back and holds his arm out to stop me in my tracks.

"No I'm serious, I am *always* here for you, like, forever and always."

I nod, "I know Crew," I half choke out a laugh and I see something in his eyes as they volley back and forth between mine. "What is it?" I say on a whisper.

"It's nothing, I just want to make sure you know I've always got you." He slowly lets his arm fall.

I feel the lump in my throat and all I can manage is a nod. He steps aside and I pull on the door, holding it open for him to follow.

"I need a minute, I actually need a piss," he shrugs, and his silly smile is back on his face in seconds.

"Okay," I laugh and let the door close as I walk to find Julian. As I approach the table, I look for Candy but she is nowhere to be seen. Pulling my chair out I smile as I catch Julian's gaze.

"Sorry about that, where were we?" I ask, my elbows on the table as I rest my chin on my linked hands and he begins chatting, picking up where we left off before we were interrupted, but Crew's words dance around in my mind for the remainder of the evening.

Chapter Seventeen

Crew

THE DRIVE HOME IS QUIET, WELL ON MY END IT IS BUT Candy has not stopped talking since we got in the car, and I am over it. Pulling up outside her apartment block I push the car into park.

"Oh," she says surprised, "I thought we were going back to yours?" I can feel her eyes burning into the side of my head, my finger drums on the steering wheel before I finally give in and look at her.

"I'm tired, I'm on an early tomorrow so I just need to get my head down..."

"Is this to do with Cody?" And hearing her name come from Candy's lips has my gut twisting and my heart sinking.

"No, Candy. It has nothing to do with Cody." Anger seeps through my pores and I close my eyes for a moment to try and contain my rage. This isn't me. I don't get angry or possessive. Or should that be I *didn't* until Cody.

Her eyes widen and I instantly feel like a prick.

"I'm sorry," and I am.

"It's fine, look, I think we just need to take a few days to cool off. You've been distracted and I know it's because you're moving away and now seeing Cody tonight has got you all riled up even though you say it's not because of her. I want this Crew, but I *need* you to want it too. I'm not up for a one sided relationship," she gives a small shrug and half a sad smile. Opening her door, she slips out before closing it and walking to my side. She stops on the pavement, and I undo my window.

"I'll wait for you Crew, you just need to know whether you are happy with *just* me." And with that she turns and unlocks her front door before slipping inside and closing me out.

———

It's Friday night and my leaving bash, well, club night. The guys are round mine and we're pre-drinking and William is half cut already. He is also celebrating as he filed for divorce from the spawn of Satan that is his wife. I shudder. She is a vile fucking woman. I have never despised a woman more than her.

"Can't believe you're leaving man," Rich wraps his arm round my shoulder and takes a sip of his beer.

"I know," I sigh.

"And you're leaving Cody here."

I nod. "And Candy it seems," and he drops his arm.

"Yeah, but Candy was just a bit of fun time right?"

"Maybe, I don't know. I did like her, but..."

"She wasn't Cody," Harry swoops in and my body vibrates to my core at the mention of her name.

"Yeah," I scoff and suddenly I want us to be off the subject.

"No one will ever be better than Cody," Will pipes up as he shoves another bottle of beer in my free hand and I take it willingly. I try to play his words down and laugh them off but it's true. No one will ever be better than Cody. Women will always compete against her whether they want to or not. That's just how it's going to be.

"Cab will be here in ten," Rich calls from downstairs and I smile to myself. Will and Harry flood out of the room and downstairs and I take this moment to just be by myself. The thought that Cody will be there tonight sends tingles down my spine, all the way to my toes. I wiggle them in my boots and glance up at my reflection in the mirror. I hope it's not awkward between me and Cody, I hope it's like old times where we can enjoy each other's company and not have to worry about competing for one another's attention. I hate that she is dating but then what did I expect by flaunting Candy in her face? Of course, she was going to retaliate, and she was allowed to date. We were just friends. Now I have Candy who would move heaven and earth for me, and I couldn't even answer her when she told me to take time.

Roughing my hand through my tousled hair, I swig my beer and swallow it down. Moving down the stairs, I threw the empty bottle in the bin and grabbed my keys. Reaching for my lightweight jacket, I shrug it on. The autumn air was beginning to nip. Ushering the guys out, I was worried William was going to get turned away because he was so pissed. I knew he was celebrating his divorce, but it was my leaving evening too and I wanted my best friends there. All of them.

TUMBLING OUT OF THE CAB WE PULL UP OUTSIDE *TAPE* in London. I haven't been here before, but Mabel hooked us up. Her husband George is a club scout, and he owns twenty percent of this club so of course, she wanted us here to support him and I was psyched. I had met George quite a bit now, we try and do group meet ups and me and Cody always act as a couple so neither of us feel left out. Neither of us ever felt like a spare wheel.

"Man, how do you deal with the nerves?" Will snuck up behind me, gripping my shoulder and giving it a squeeze. I turn and look at him.

"Nerves?"

"Yeah, like, I am pretty sure I have a belly full of butter-flies at the thought of seeing Hallie," he says, and I smirk.

"I don't deal with them. I have them turning and knot-ting my stomach now at the thought of seeing her again." I inhale, "But I bury them down, try and block them out. You'll get there." I nudge into him. "But don't be nervous man. She's currently filing for divorce too..." I smile and he smiles at me, his grip tightening into my shoulder. I chuckle and I feel her, my heart racing as if I was on speed. Turning, I see the three of them strutting towards us and I swear I have a hard on as soon as I lay eyes on her. She is wearing an ice blue midi dress, the small beads and crystals glistening in the moonlight. My jaw lax, my eyes lighting up and my lips curl into a smile. She looks like a fucking angel. My *guardian* angel. Her plump lips split as she bares her white, perfectly straight teeth. Her icy blue eyes are glued to mine and fuck, I miss those eyes.

Her arms hang around my neck as she places a soft kiss on my cheek then she moves to Will, Richard and Harry. I don't like it. I want her back.

Will is like a giddy schoolboy when he sees Hallie and I must say, her and Mabel look stunning, but they have nothing on my Cody. She is phenomenal. *My baby.*

The cold air nips at our skin and I see Cody shudder.

Shrugging my coat off I rest it on her shoulders then link my fingers through hers. This feels so right. Leading her forward but following Mabel who says something to the guy on the door and he gives her a wink. We all follow behind her into the neon bright room. A large catwalk illuminated in red neon takes focal point of the room, but it's not till we get closer that it's a centre between the backs of chesterfield style leather booth areas with what looks like glass cages for dancing. Mabel squeals as she sees George and throws herself at him as we're taking off to a red roped area.

The club is heaving, and the music is pumping through the speakers vibrating through my body. There is a certain type of people here, we were in Mayfair. I did feel out of place but once I have some alcohol swimming through my veins I will settle. I let go of Cody's hand as she steps into the area that George has led us too. I step up and George pats me on the back.

"Thanks for hooking us up with this, man," I smile and reach for his hand to shake.

"Only the best for you, my dude." I sit opposite Cody as she settles herself between Mabel and Hallie and the guys fall down around us in the spare seats. Of course, I had Will next to me. He was obviously feeling a little overwhelmed. He has been married for as long as I could remember and now, he was technically single sitting opposite a woman he has a massive crush on. I smirk as George re-appears with two magnum bottles of vodka and champagne. *Shit man, my head is going to be a mess tomorrow.* That thought is soon pushed out of my head as Mabel pours us all a glass of champagne and stands to toast.

"To friends, one is moving away, one is getting divorced, and one is divorced as of tonight," she cheers and shouts over the music and I see Hallie's eyes widen before they lock with William's. I quickly turn my head not wanting to intrude on their private and intimate eye fuckery that's going on. I scoff, holding my glass up and clinking them in the middle of the table.

WE WERE ALL ON THE DANCE FLOOR BUSTING OUR BEST moves and we were too wankered to give two shits about what we looked like to the other club goers, but to us? We were having the best time. I still slightly, swaying from foot to foot as the music dies down and a new beat starts and I stop. My eyes lift and find hers. She looks so carefree as she sways her hips, holding her arms above her head and moves to the steady beat. It takes her a moment or two to realise the song and that's when she finds me. Seeking me out. *More Than Friends – James Hype* and I swear this song was written for us. Cody stands, pointing at me as she begins to mouth the words until the beat drops and she is jumping and thrashing around. I swallow down the thickness in my throat.

I listen to the words and fuck, I feel them. Every single one of them. I move towards her and suddenly, everything feels like it's moving in slow motion. It's only me and her. Her brown hair is swooshing around her, her hips circling and grinding as her arms go high only to feel down her curves. As I close the gap, she turns and gives me the perfect view of her peachy arse. I still, inches away from her body. The body I have so desperately wanted to touch, to hold, to cherish and now, I don't know if I can do it. I am fixated and fascinated by the way she moves. I lose all control by the chorus and my large, thick arms snake round her tiny waist and that's when she does it. Her arse grinding on my throbbing, bulging cock.

"Petal," I rasp as my lips brush against the shell of her ear, her head tipping back against my chest.

"Yes, big man?" She purrs and I groan.

"I need you to stop dry humping me with your bum." I suck my bottom lip in then sink my teeth into it as I hold my breath.

"But you feel so good," she turns her head to speak the words against my chin. My fingers dig into the thin material of her dress as she dances, and I begin to move with her.

"Petal," I whisper, as the music begins to die down.

"Yes," she's breathless.

"Are you with Julian?" I hate to even ask, but I needed to know. I am no cheater. She shakes her head before spinning round to face me.

"Candy?"

I shake my head from side to side, "No, she told me to think my shit over and let her know my decision..." I trail of as our eyes bounce back and forth with each other's. "What's it going to be..." I smirk, my arms tightening around her as I pull her tiny frame flush with my bigger body.

"Take me home, big boy."

Fuck.

Chapter Eighteen

Cody

THIS IS WHAT HAPPENS WHEN YOU MIX ALCOHOL WITH your best boy friend. Lines that were once so thick and bold were now beginning to blur into nothing. Anxiety starts to pump through my veins at the thought of me not performing. I am hard to get off, I know that, everyone knows that. What if Crew is the same and he just pump pump squirts then rolls over and falls asleep. Oh god. Please no. I close my eyes and silently pray to all the gods that Crew is one of the very few, and I mean few that have made me cum. Crew's hands have been nestled between my thighs, drawing and trailing his fingers in small shapes each time edging closer to the apex of my thighs. My sex aches, my belly tight and full of knots and I so desperately need the release.

The taxi rolls to a stop and Crew taps his phone to pay. Opening the door, he takes my hand and leads me out onto the pavement.

"You okay?" He asks, his thumb brushing over my bottom lip and pulling it down as he sucks in a breath. I nod, because it's the truth. I am okay.

Tugging him towards my front door, I fumble to find the keys and unlock it. Stepping inside I throw my bag down and lock us both in. I need a drink.

"Drink?" I ask sheepishly as I begin to walk down towards the kitchen.

"Damn, am I that bad that you need your beer goggles on?" He scoffs as he follows me, and I suddenly realise how bad that must've sounded to him.

I turn, eyes widening, and I shake my head. "No, no... it's for me, for my own anxiety."

His thick brow pops up causing his forehead to crease as he listens. I knot my fingers together then rub my sweaty palms down my thighs. *Stunning.*

"Care to explain?" He licks his lips and smirks at me.

"I'm hard to get off..." I blurt out, slapping my hand across my mouth.

"I don't believe that for a second," he shakes his head and begins to close the gap between us and I don't move back.

"It's true, I've told you about my past with hoppys... they come and bang me then leave because they can't fulfil me. I'm not one of these girls that literally gets touched and comes. I don't come through penetrative sex. I normally have to get myself off while... Well, you know."

"And what's wrong with that?"

"Well, men don't like it, they want to be the one to make me orgasm, not me making it by myself," I blush under his firing line of questions. "So now I just fake it, so they leave quicker..." I whisper against his lips as he hovers his over mine.

"Baby, you just haven't been with anyone who was willing to take the time to worship you like you deserve."

My breath is snatched as he crashes his lips into mine,

my heart racing as his tongue sweeps through my parted lips and I melt into him. His arms wrap tighter around me as he holds me up because I feel like my legs are about to buckle under me. His kiss intensifies and it feels electrifying, the soberness in me slowly drifting away as I am drunk off just him. My fingers clutch his tee as I hold him with all I have because I am *that* desperate for him. He breaks away and I swear I gasp; the air being knocked from my lungs as I crave his kiss as if he is my only form of oxygen.

"Should we be doing this while you're so intoxicated?" He whispers.

"I'm not that drunk," I breathe. The taxi drive and realisation of what we were about to do sobered me up.

He smirks, pulling me closer.

A nervous laugh bubbles out of me as my fingers brush against my lips and I feel the tingle shoot through to my core. My lips feel bruised but in the best possible way. He exhales, his eyes pinned to mine and his fingers brush against my cheek. *Is he having second thoughts?*

He lets his fingers skim past my jaw and onto my shoulder when I am spun round so my back is against him. I feel his lips at the shell of my ear and his shaky breath makes my skin erupts into goosebumps.

"I think the problem is..." he trails off for a moment as his fingertips skim up the side of my neck then dust down over my collar bone, "no man has spent enough time getting to know your body," I hitch in a breath as the hand that is splayed flat against my stomach begins a slow descent towards the curve of my hip, squeezing and pushing me into him where I can feel his erection. "I will know every mark, every scar, every imperfection on your skin by the time I am finished," he whispers as he moves his fingertips over to the other side of my neck, repeating the same trail. "You just need to be worked up in the right way, your senses need to be woken so by the time I fill you with my cock you're ready to explode." He smiles against the shell of my ear and my head tips back as his dirty words make my stomach knot and clench my sex. The hand that is curled around my hip skims down to my thigh, his fingers running across the hem of my dress and delicately tracing over my bare skin. Doubt begins to fill me that I won't perform like he wants me to. I stiffen slightly and he feels it.

"You need to get out of your head, live in the moment, *feel* what you're doing to me, what *I am* doing to you." His fingers slip under the hem of my blue dress and skims higher up my thigh. "Was you even wet when those poor excuses of men touched you?" His voice is thick and tight, I can feel his jaw clenching against my skin.

I shake my head, and I feel a lump forming in my throat and a hot tear rolls down my cheek as I close my eyes, the realisation hitting me like a freight train. I'm not sad, it's just hit me at how much I desperately love this man.

"I've got you," his voice is raspy as he glides his fingers through the thin material of my thong and I quiver in his grasp. A primal growl leaves him as he feels me through the material and his hand slips out of my dress and he pushes my dress up round my waist. My hand clutches onto the hem of his tee as I feel his fingers slide my thong to the side and exposing me. He slowly runs one of his fingers through my folds then rims the tip of his finger at my entrance.

"I can feel your arousal, your wet for me petal," he whispers as I feel his hands lift off my body. I nervously push my dress back over my hips. My cheeks blush and I suddenly feel self-conscious.

He tuts, shaking his head. He steps forward and takes my shaking hand into his.

"I am nowhere near finished with you yet. Let me take you to bed." One side of his lip lifts as he smirks, and I nod. *Jesus Christ, why does he make me feel like this?*

And instead of me leading the way to my room, he leads me, and I follow like a lost fucking puppy.

But that's just it.

I feel lost around him. But not in a bad way, in the best fucking way. I seek him out, he seeks me. He is my anchor, keeping me grounded and when I am with him, I will never be lost for long. Because he is my home.

Chapter Nineteen

Standing at the foot of my bed, Crew closes the door and I smile. "You know..." I stall for a moment as he takes a step towards me, and his scent intoxicates me. "I only wore this dress for you," I nibble my bottom lip as I let my eyes fall to the floor.

"Did you now?" And he falls back slightly as he looks me up and down, admiring my attire. "Well, it's a real damn shame that I am going to rip it from your body because I need to see you, I need to feel your skin under my fingertips."

I giggle. "How about I take it off, you sit at the edge of the bed big boy, I'll give you a little show." I am internally cringing; this is not who I am. What the hell have you done with Cody? My subconscious is yelling at me.

He wraps his arm around my waist, pulling me into him and tugs on my bottom lip. "I cannot wait to sink my teeth into this a little later," he winks then shoves me onto the bed and laughs.

"Idiot," I call out as I push up, "you're meant to be the

one sitting on the bed," I tsk and he nods, spinning me round him so he takes my place. He shuffles around then lays back slightly, propping himself up on his elbows.

"Comfortable?" I smirk, hands on my hips.

"Oh, yes," he nods firmly.

Knotting my fingers, I shy away slightly, and he notices. Of course, he does. I swear this man knows me better than myself.

"Eyes on me princess, it's only me and you." He hums.

I close my eyes for a second and inhale deeply before I focus on him and only him. I smirk when I see his eyes falling to the hem of my dress as he waits for me, anticipation flashing on his face. Suddenly, I hear the song playing in my head and I know I need to put it on. This is how I would imagine it would play out if we were in a movie, me about to take my dress off and the song playing over the top. I hold my finger up and run to my iPad that is sitting on the bedside table, he sits up and his eyes follow me round the room. I unlock it and find the song I wanted then turn and head back to the foot of the bed, the sound of Dress – Taylor Swift fills the room. My confidence blooms as I listen to the queen that is Taylor. Everything she is singing is what I want to shout to Crew, to tell him this is how I feel. All of this is for him. The smiles, the laughs, the tears, the nervousness, the shy little girl who begs to come out. Every single part is for him. Three words. Three words that could change the course of this evening, the course of our lives... I bite my tongue on them though and get my head back into the moment. Our moment.

Exhaling, I grip the hem of my dress and slip it over my hips, and I hear the suck of breath that he inhales.

"Fuck," the groan that leaves him is glutaral and sexy as

sin. I smirk. Lifting it over my head, I hold it out to the side of me and wink as I drop it to the floor.

"Oh, you sexy fucking minx, get over here," he laughs, holding his needy grabby hands towards me and I stumble back laughing.

"Not so easy," I frown and kick my shoes off.

"Is this how you're gonna play it? Slow and sensual and tease me till my balls constrict and blow?"

I shrug, "Maybe." My tongue darts out and coats my top lip slowly as I refuse to pull my eyes from him and suddenly, I don't feel nervous anymore. The way he is devouring me with his eyes makes me feel bold and brazen and I am here for it. Reaching behind me, I unclasp my bra and let it fall. His eyes fall to my heaving chest, and I basically melt when he tugs and pulls his bottom lip between his teeth.

"Please, fuck, Cody..." Begging, he shuffles closer to the edge of the bed.

I step cautiously towards him, giving him what he craves and feeding his addiction as well as mine.

He encases my waist in his arms, his head tips back and his brown, wide eye penetrate through mine and my heart races. The spell that he holds me under is broken quickly when I feel his lips trailing soft, butterfly kisses along my navel, his tongue dipping into my belly button. Normally, if a hoppy done that to me, I would be grossed out and out of the moment like a bat out of hell. But Crew? No chance of that. I was a sucker for this man.

Hook. Line. Sinker.

His hands creep up my back, stopping at my ribs as he pushes me forward and closer to him. I watch as his mouth nips and sucks over my sensitive skin. I breathe out, my hands losing their selves in his brown hair, I tug and drag his head back as I lean over and cover his mouth with mine. I need him like the oxygen I breathe. My tongue dips into his mouth as our kiss deepens and my stomach tightens as I feel the ache between my legs, my sex throbbing with need and want. I feel the clench of his fingers in my cheeks as he hollows my mouth and pulls away but not before sinking his teeth into my bottom lip and sucking on it. I whimper, fluttering my eyes open to be met with his steady gaze.

He smirks and I know that smirk. It's his 'I'm up to something' smirk. Before I can ask, his tongue flicks across my hardened nipple, his large hand kneading and groping me as he sucks me into his mouth. The pinch of pain shoots through me then pleasures swarms me in an instant. Popping my nipple from his mouth, he blows warm air over me then moves his delicious mouth to cover the other side. I let my head fall back, his spare hand slipping round my waist as he squeezes whilst his mouth and hand assault me with pleasure. He pushes me back, breaking away as he stands and looks down at me.

"Get on the bed, legs open," he orders but his tone is soft, and he leans in and kisses me on the forehead, lingering slightly. He steps to the side, and I crawl up the bed towards the wooden headboard and I flip over so my back is against the surface, and I do as he says, I let my legs fall open. Kneeling on the bed, he crawls towards me and reaches for my face, squeezing my cheeks with little force and hovers his lips over mine and he smiles, his eyes darkening if that's even possible. "You're such a good fucking girl."

I fucking swear I just got fanny flutters. I didn't even think it was a thing?!

Praise. New kink: unlocked.

Dropping my cheeks from his grasp I exhale on a shaky

breath as I watch him with intent. I can't read him, I have no idea what he is thinking which only turns me on so much more. Shuffling back, his fingers hook into the side of my knickers, tugging them down. I lift my hips up so he can pull them off. His ablaze blue eyes flick with excitement and anticipation as he brings them to his nose and inhales. He winks, licking his lips before shoving them into the back pocket of his jeans. I lunge forward, grabbing the hem of his tee and push onto my knees so I can pull it over his head. I need to see him. All of him.

"Patience is a virtue, princess." He clicks his tongue to the roof of his mouth and his cockiness is only making me more impatient. His fingers wrap round my wrist, and he shakes his head, "We're not there yet, baby."

I frown, and I'm pushed back. I pant, laying here completely naked underneath him. He drops to all fours, edging closer to me. "Back to the headboard, sit up."

I do as he says.

"Now, my little dove. I want you to touch yourself, show me how you like to be touched. I want to know what gets you off. I want you at the point of fucking begging. And I swear to you princess, you'll be begging, and as soon as I sink my cock into your hot, wet, pussy you'll explode."

My chest is heaving up and down as I try and control my breathing. Damn it, Crew is filthy.

Leaning down, his lips are hovering over mine and his stare on me is intense.

"Now, I am going to see how wet you are," he kneels back, his eyes falling between my legs. Gliding his finger through my folds he grins like the Cheshire cat who got the cream. Swirling his fingers at my opening, I gasp at the feeling of him teasing the tip before pulling out.

"You're so wet, touch yourself baby. Show me how to work you."

My hand trembles as I grab and squeeze my heavy breast, kneading to find some sort of release from the teasing and torment that I am feeling. I let my free hand skim over my body, my fingers tracing across my belly before I let them dip between my legs. My breath catches at the back of my throat when I feel just how wet I am. Rubbing over my swollen and sensitive clit I find the courage to lift my eyes to steady them on Crew as he watches me touch myself.

"Fuck, baby... you look so fucking hot." He shuffles, kneeling up and unbuttons the buttons on his flies of his jeans and I am silently begging that he touches himself, I want to see him.

Slipping my finger from my clit, I let them glide into my folds then dip a finger inside the hot, wetness of my pussy. I gasp then rub my clit harder while dipping the tip of a finger in and out, edging and teasing myself as my orgasm teeters on the edge.

"So you like edging," he rasps, palming himself through the thick material of his jeans. Closing my eyes, I sink my head back into the pillow as I immerse myself in pleasuring myself. I feel the bed dip and I feel him over me as he snatches my hand away. "Keep touching your clit, I need to feel you." And I clench, my head falling forward, my chin down as I watch myself. Shit.

Two of his fingers swirl in my arousal, gently nudging them into me slightly before pulling them back.

"Your sweet pussy is dripping." He licks his lips as he pushes them a little deeper this time, holding them until he feels the tightness of my clench. Smirking, he gently wraps his fingers around the base of my throat. "How about being choked, petal? Does that do anything for you?" he asks, his two thick fingers pushing deeper and curling.

"Crew," I whisper, just as he edges them back out again and I can hear just how wet I am.

"It seems you're learning more about yourself as well as me," he kisses my lips softly, his tongue swiping across my bottom lip as he begins to fuck me with his fingers.

Now, this is what sex should feel like.

Chapter Twenty

Crew

I FEEL LIKE I HAVE DIED AND GONE TO HEAVEN. SHE IS everything I ever dreamed of and more. She's grinding her hips down onto my fingers as I fuck her with them, her arousal is running down my knuckles and I am so turned on.

"Crew," she moans out as her fingers circle over her clit slowly, sweat beads her skin as she works herself up towards her orgasm.

My eyes move from her face to her tight little cunt, and I can't stop watching as she takes me, clenching around me. And suddenly, I am famished. Slipping my fingers from her, my hands curve over her hips and I lift them, bringing her sweet as fuck pussy higher.

"Crew," her eyes widen in panic, but I ignore her as I cover her sex with my mouth, sucking on her swollen clit making her hips buck forward. I smirk against her as my tongue swipes over her bud, twirling and swirling then gliding it through her slick folds. Plunging my tongue into her pussy I eat her as if she was my last meal and I was fucking starving.

"Fuck," she whispers, and I watch her through my

lashes, her fingers pinching and twisting her nipples to heighten her pleasure as her hips gyrate against my face, gaining the friction she so desperately craves. I groan with a mouthful of her then ripple my tongue over her clit. I still, sitting back and lowering her hips back onto the bed.

"Crew, what's, what's wrong..." the panic is evident in her voice and my eyes glower over her, a smirk pinching at my lips as I grab her hips and flip her on her belly which causes a screech. I laugh, lifting her peachy arse in the air and then I stare, only for a moment as I watch her pussy glistening and I'm ready to feast on her again. Rearing forward, I lower my top half and slip my tongue into her opening as I fuck her with it, my hand tucking round her hip as I slap her clit and rub gently.

Her legs buckle slightly but she pushes up on her hands, so she is on all fours. I groan as she makes it harder. I stop, lay on my back and reach up for her hips as I slam her down on top of me. Wiggling my brows, her eyes widen in horror.

"Jesus, no, no Crew," she pants, "I'll suffocate you," and I belly laugh.

"Oh baby, it would be my honour to die with your pussy on my face..." I smirk, "at least I'll know I've done my job right," and before I can give her a chance to argue back, I flick my tongue against her clit and rock her hips over my face. Her hands are in her hair, grabbing at the root as she rocks her hips voluntarily now.

"Crew," she pants, her head falling forward as our eyes connect. "I need more, baby, I need more," she begs, and I know what she needs. Using my hand to push her bum, I make her fall forward, so she is on all fours over me, her pussy still where I want it over my mouth. Spreading her bum cheeks, I dip my finger into her cunt, swirling in her wetness before running my finger over her pert asshole, pressing softly against it as I do to coat it in her arousal. She stills but I continue to push one finger in her tight hole and plunge another into her soaked pussy filling her to the hilt. This is what she *needs*.

Her hips rock back and forth as she takes what she needs, fucking my fingers until her movements become more lazy, slow and her body begins to tremble. Sucking on her clit, I lick hard and slow but fuck her hard with my fingers and her whole body convulses as she falls forward, crying out as she orgasms, her pussy clenching around me. Pulling my fingers from her, I slide her back to sitting over me and I drink every ounce of her as she comes all over my tongue.

Chapter Twenty-One

Cody

EVERY PART OF MY BODY IS TINGLING. EVERY PART OF me is over sensitised and I am fucking spent. I tremble on all fours as I slowly come down from the best orgasm I have ever had. Crew worked me in ways I never knew I needed or wanted. He gently rolls me on my back, his hand splayed across my stomach and his other hand props his head up as he lays on his side. I lean up and kiss him, tasting my arousal on his tongue. His tongue dips deeper into my mouth, caressing my mouth as he groans. I pull away, sitting up and tugging the bed sheet with me.

"I'm sorry I took so long," I nibble my bottom lip as I let my eyes slip closed when I feel his thumb and finger on my chin, tilting it up so I have no choice but to look up to him.

"Don't ever fucking apologise. I get off on getting you off. I would rather spend hours making you come then you making me," he smiles, "but, that being said, I am desperate to sink myself inside of you."

My cheeks pinch with a blush as I tighten the sheet around me.

"Give me five, just need the loo," I rub my lips together

and hop up off the bed when the sheet is tugged out of my grip. I cover my boobs with my arm and clasp my hand over my sex as I turn.

"Crew!"

"Baby, don't hide now. You've not long cum all over my face, tongue and fingers. I've seen it all. All I have to do is close my eyes and see it whenever I want," he wiggles is eyebrows. Rolling my eyes, I laugh and that's when I see just how hard he is. He is *solid*. Rushing for the loo, I close the door and take a breather. I am craving him, what he done to me in there was indescribable and even when he went to the place no man has ever been before gave me thrills.

Leaning over the sink I splash my face with cold water. Slowly rolling myself up I look at myself in the mirror. I have a glow about me, sure it could be a post orgasm glow but I'll take it. It's a glow I've not seen for a very long while. Unwrapping my fingers from the edge of the sink I bend and grab a condom from the bathroom cabinet. I'm clean, I always use condoms and get checked every few months and I even have added bonus of birth control, but I don't want to assume that Crew would be okay with that. He knows my past and I am sure I surpass his bed numbers. Flipping the foil packet between my fingers I open the door slowly and my eyes widen as I see Crew laying on my bed, completely naked, smiling at me. My eyes slowly move from his face to his dick that is resting on his stomach and all I can think is RIP Vagina.

Crew

She exits the bathroom and stops dead in her tracks but stumbles as she does. Her eyes are wide, and I know she is taking every *inch* of me in. I smile at her before I let my eyes trail over her fucking amazing body. I feel the strain against my cock as it bobs, pre cum sitting at the tip.

Calling her over with my finger, I can see the self-consciousness blanketing her again. I'm not having it, I'm not letting her lose herself in her head.

She moves towards me, and I see the flash of silver sitting at the tip of her fingers. I am so desperate to feel her bare, to let her feel every inch of me but I suppose she doesn't know where I have been, we need to be sensible. Safe. Not to get caught up in the moment but fuck I want to. I groan as I begin to fist myself slowly and as soon as she is near the bed, I reach up and grab her, pulling her on top of me. A shy giggle comes out of her as she throws her hands over her face.

I wrap my fingers round her wrist and tug her hands away from her and smile. "No hiding baby," I state, winking, "I've seen it all, don't shy away from me now." Clasping my hand round the base of her throat, I pull her towards me and sink my tongue inside her lips while my other hand roams down her body, rounding the curve of her ass. Smiling against her mouth, I push two fingers inside of her, her pussy clenching round me. Breaking away, I push her up as I continue to fuck her with my fingers. "Now," I smirk as her eyes pin to mine, "you're going to ride my cock until you're spent, I want you to use my body like your play-ground. Use it in whatever way you *need* to get yourself off because baby, the end game is you coming over my cock."

"Crew," she breathes as I feel her pussy tightening with her clenches.

"I got you baby," I whisper, pulling my fingers out of her then push them between my lips, rolling my eyes in the back of my head as I enjoy her taste. My heavy hands move to her hips as I grasp her skin tightly, lifting her.

"Condom," she breathes on shaky breath, "Crew, we need..."

"I know princess, I know," I soothe as my eyes fall between our bodies, rounding one of my hands round her hips I splay it against her warm skin on her stomach and push her back slightly to see her glistening cunt. Sucking in a breath, I swipe my fingers through her folds and rub them at the tip of my cock and groan. I feel like I am ready to explode, but I need to hold out for her. I feel her eyes burning into me which makes me lift my eyes and I see a glint of darkness in them. Her mind is ticking.

She leans over me, pressing her full tits against my chest and lowers her lips to the shell of my ear. "I can't wait for your thick cock to stretch and fill my pussy, I want to feel the sting and ache tomorrow as I enjoy my day knowing you're going to be on my mind because you were the one to do it to me."

Her fingers dance down my side before she lifts her ass in the air, her hand wrapping round the base of my cock.

"And here I was thinking you were all shy, my little dove."

She blushes, shaking her head from side to side. "What can I say, you seem to bring the dirty side out in me," and I groan as she flicks her tongue round the shell of my ear then sucks on my ear lobe. She presses up slightly, then runs the head of my cock through her slick folds. My head tips back, her hips rolling as she rocks her soaked pussy over my length and the whole time her fucking ice blues are pene-trating me. Bucking my hips up, I feel my orgasm creeping closer and I know that I am not going to be able to hold off. My hand flies to her throat, pushing her so she is sitting up on top of me and I fist myself, pumping and pressing my tip into her clit.

"You want to tease me baby? I'll tease you back," I grit, tightening my grip round her throat and she fucking smiles at me. "Fuck," I call out, bucking forward and moving my cock from her hot pussy and watch as I spurt cum over her stomach.

She climbs off me and smirks like the cat that got the fucking cream. I puff, rolling on my side and propping my head on my hand.

"Well, aren't you a little fuck tease," I smirk as she pulls her sheets over her body to cover herself.

I shake my head from side to side and tsk, bunching the sheet in my hand and tug it away from her.

"I thought you would have been done now, big boy."

"Well, princess, you're mistaken." I wink and reach for her, grabbing her and pulling her down onto me, a small gasp leaving when she feels my cock hardening underneath her.

"Now, like I said before you teased me into coming, use my body. Fuck me until you're ready to explode," I turn my head, reaching for the foil packet and splitting it open. "Lift up," I tap her ass and she does as I ask, rolling the condom down my length. "Fucking hate these things," I groan.

"I know, but we need to be safe..." she half smiles and I feel like she feels like I need the condom more than her. Holding her in place, I shuffle up the bed and sit against the headboard.

"Turn round," I twirl my finger and she spins, her legs resting either side of my thick thighs.

My fingers skim round her hip and stroke over her swollen clit. Her head falls back against my chest and I pin her there with my fingers wrapped around her throat. "This is how I am going to fuck you, I want you to work me how you need me okay?"

"Yes,' she rasps as I slip my fingers into her soaked pussy, stretching her with three.

"So fucking wet," I groan, nipping her neck with my teeth wanting to mark her. Pulling my fingers from her, I fist the base of my cock and push her forward. She steadies herself, lifting herself up as I line the girthy tip of my cock at her opening and nudge. She clenches, tensing.

"Relax baby, let me in. I promise I'll feel amazing," I smile, licking my lips and already I am having to hold back because I feel like I am ready to explode all over again.

Spreading her legs further, she lowers slightly as she takes more of me. Inch by inch I fill her to the hilt. The gasp that leaves her makes my cock throb and pulse inside of her. I am desperate to move, but she's in charge. She is taking the reins. I want her to take everything from me. She takes a moment as if trying to adjust to the thickness of me and I gently rock up, getting the urge to move. I *needed* to move. My fingers dig into the skin of her hips as I lift her off me slightly then slam her back down.

"Move baby, I need you to move," my voice is practically a beg.

"Crew," she pants as her hips rock forward slowly as she takes me deeper.

"That's it baby, take everything you need and *want* from me."

Her head tips back, as I let one of my hands roam up

her body, twisting and pulling her nipple as I pass then place my hand at the base of her neck where it belongs. After a moment or two, she brings her knees up so she is in a crouching position, her hands resting behind her on my stomach as she lifts herself up and down my cock, bringing me out to the tip then sliding back down and filling herself.

"Jesus, Cody," I pant, both hands back on her hips as I guide her up and down faster now. I feel her clench and tighten around me.

"Crew, I need more," she cries as my fingers slap on her clit, rubbing fast as she continues to ride me.

Growling, I push her forward onto all fours and kneel behind her. I don't give her a moment before I am slamming myself inside of her, hard and fast.

"Yes," she moans out as I fist her brown hair, tugging her up as I ride her, my spare hand slapping her ass cheek then pushing a finger inside her slit while her cunt is full of my cock. I drag my bottom lip between my teeth when I see her arousal smeared round her and dripping down her legs. Pulling my finger out, I rub it round her tight arsehole and plunge my thumb inside while my cock works her up to where she needs to be.

She's moaning out, her pussy clenching and I can feel my own orgasm teetering. Her hand moves to her clit as she pleasures herself, my thumb slipping in and out of her tight arsehole at the same speed as my cock. My eyes fall as I watch how her perfect pussy stretches around me, looking as if she is ready to split at any minute.

"I'm getting close, oh, Crew, please," she cries out, our skin slapping together. I slow and pull myself to the tip and I feel her body shudder as her orgasm begins to build as I push back into her hard.

"Do it again," she whispers, her body beginning to tremble.

Pulling back I hold it, the tip of my cock just inside her pussy. She's rubbing and working her clit fast. I line the tip of my finger up above my cock at her entrance and push both of them in at the same time which make her cry out, jolting forward.

"Fuck me," I groan, tipping my head back as her hips ride back and forth up and down my cock and finger. "Such a good girl, keep fucking me, shit," I grit, snapping my head forward and watching as I push her closer to her impending orgasm.

"I'm going to come," she moans as her whole body shakes and her pussy tightens like a vice around me as her muscles contract and I come with her, our cries filling the room.

———

"Veto," she says breathlessly.

I snap my head up and look at her, my brows are furrowed as I let the words sink in.

"Veto!?" I grit, "damn, I've never been vetoed after sex before," I smirk and her head turns to face me, her blues widening at me.

"Oh my god, no!" She gasps, "The nickname!!"

"What one!?"

"Princess."

"Oh, thank fuck," I place my hand on my chest in relief and fall back into her pillows. "I was having a mini panic attack that you were about to *veto* our session."

She laughs and pulls the sheet under her chin.

The air crackles between us, the tension growing minute by minute as words go unspoken.

"Are you all ready to leave tomorrow?" She asks, turning her head on the pillow to face me.

Facing her, I let my eyes trail over her face making sure I remember every single feature of her.

"I think so, just about anyway," I laugh but my stomach knots in uneasiness, anxiety plaguing me at the thought of leaving her tomorrow. My heart sinks when the reality hits me in the face like a shovel, I had fallen so fucking hard for her and us having this *goodbye* only cemented the fact that I was head over heels in love with her.

Chapter Twenty-Two

Cody

STRETCHING UP IN BED, MY WHOLE BODY ACHES AND reminds me of last night which I spent with Crew. My heart constricts and my stomach knots knowing that he leaves today. That he leaves me today. The three words are on the tip of my tongue, I have fallen so hard for Crew but he has made it obvious that he doesn't feel the same despite the attraction between us last night. We're in the friend zone, we both put each other there and we were in too deep to be able pull each other out of it. I roll on my side, a delicious sting coursing through me as I move, reminding me that he was there. The breaths were passing his lips softly and I could honestly lay and watch him all day. His eyes spring open, and it takes him a moment or two to realise where he is. His head turns and I can see the relaxation washing over his face instantly.

"Morning," I smile, propped on my elbow, my hand resting on my head as I smile like a goofball at him.

"Morning love," the intimate nickname makes my insides burn; his voice is raspy and rough from sleep, but he still sounds delicious as hell.

"Sleep, okay?" I ask, clenching my thighs when I see him in all his glory this morning.

"Like a fucking log, you?"

"Yeah, I slept good." Beaming, I roll onto my back and pick the skin round my nail bed. *I can't believe he is leaving.*

"I'm going to miss you honey bun," he croons.

"I'm going to miss you too, *fuzzy butt*." My heart hurts. "But one thing I'm not going to miss is your cheesy nicknames." I nudge him with my elbow.

"Oh, stop it petal, you know you are," he rolls towards me and lays his heavy arm over my body as he pulls me towards him. He nuzzles into the crook of my neck and inhales my scent and my insides coil. I don't want him to leave. *Ever.*

No words are spoken, we just lay in the silence and enjoy every single minute of this moment.

Crew

I leave her in bed as I walk downstairs into the kitchen with just my towel wrapped round my waist. We had showered together, and I thought I would give her a minute or two to have some space to process her thoughts. The words sat on the tip of my tongue, I was desperate to call and cancel the move and the promotion, but I couldn't. I had to take this; she would be so mad at me if I didn't.

I shake the thoughts from my head and waltz to flick the coffee machine on, turning I switch on the radio and smile. Whistling and humming along to *Just can't get enough – The Saturdays* that was playing, I rummage around and find two cups. I was so engrossed in the music, breaking out in song that I freeze when I turn to seeing Hallie standing in front of me. Eyes wide, jaw lax and frozen to the spot.

"Well, good morning, Hallie," I beam at her, and she tightens her grip on the keys that she is holding.

"Crew?" She gasps.

"Yup, why, who else would it be?" I wiggle my brows.

"No one," she shakes her head, her body slowly relaxing, "I just wasn't expecting you, that's all."

"Cody is just getting dressed..." I take a moment to look down at myself and smirk as my eyes find her.

"Did you and her..." she pauses, pointing her finger at me then letting her eyes fall to my waist then meet my gaze.

"What do you think?" I ask, grazing my fingers through my messy hair.

"Cody!" She calls as he runs for the stairs, and I belly laugh.

"I'll make you a cup of coffee sweet cheeks!" I call after her.

Cody

Towel drying my hair, I let my mind wander to the night before and I still feel like I am on cloud nine. Crew delivered on his promise of working me until I came. No man has ever, and I mean *ever* spent the time on my body that Crew did last night. My heart flutters and I stare dreamily into the distance when my bedroom door bangs open to see a flustered Hallie. *Shit*. I forgot she was popping in this morning.

"Morning," I chirped, fidgeting round with my skin care bottles to keep my hands busy.

"*Really?*" She storms towards me and sits on the bed then looks over her shoulder and jumps up in disgust.

"It was sort of like a goodbye... ya know?" A nervous giggle leaves me and Jesus, the nerves were crashing through me.

"A goodbye?"

"Yes," I snapped, turning to face her from my dressing table, "a goodbye because Hallie, as you know, I am stupidly in love with that man, and he doesn't feel the same. So just to have something from him, *anything*. The way he made me feel last night was the best goodbye present he could have given me. Don't judge me, you have no right to judge me. Was it stupid? Yes. Did I cross a fucking line? Yes. But honestly, the lines are blurring around me because I can't decipher my feelings. I want to shout out at him, tell him how I feel but I can't, because he *does not* feel the same as me." I puff, I'm panting, and my eyes are stinging as I try to hold off the tears. Swallowing the lump down and shaking my head from side to side. She doesn't get it.

Pumping my day cream onto the back of my hand I rub it into my cheeks and cover the rest of my face as Hallie just stands there too stunned to speak.

Throwing my tube of product down, I grab my brush and angrily brush it through the ends of my hair as I fester on my own words and thoughts.

"Cody, I didn't mean..."

"Of course, you did," I shrug my shoulders up and turn to face her. "Do you know how shit I feel about it all?" My brows lift in question.

"I get it, I do..."

"Do you? Because you came across really judgemental and that isn't my best friend. I would expect that from Mabel, but not from *you*. You know everything about me,

153

everything to do with my feelings for that man. I have craved him for so long and he finally gave in. I *finally* gave in. And do you know what Hallie?" I pause waiting for her to speak but she just shakes her head from side to side softly, "It felt *so fucking good*. I have never been treated the way that Crew treated me last night. He made me feel like a queen and even if it was just sex, it was the best fucking sex I have ever had."

She steps towards me, her hand resting on my shoulder softly, "I just don't want you getting hurt," she whispers, squeezing.

"How can I get hurt any more when I am already dying on the inside that he is leaving, that this is all we'll ever be, all we will ever have? It kills me that we will never be more than *this*." I swallow and I feel the needles at the back of my eyes, tears pricking and that's when Hallie encases me in her arms. I hear the sigh that leaves her as she holds me while I sob.

I AM FINISHING MY MAKE-UP WHEN CREW WALKS IN with three coffees and toast. I turn to face him and smile, chocking on a laugh that he is still wrapped in his bath towel. He passes Hallie her coffee with a cautious look, then turns to me.

"Here we go, butterscotch." I take it and smile.

"Veto." I roll my eyes and take a mouthful.

"Sorry it took me forever..." he stills, "okay, it didn't take me forever. I wanted to give you two a minute because by the look on Hallie's face, she was either going to murder me or make sure I hadn't murdered you." He steps back and sits on the bed next to Hallie.

"I hope this bed has been disinfected," she smirks and

nudges into Crew, "what time are you heading out, I spoke to Will..." she stalls.

"We both know you and Will have a little something going on, this is a safe space, you can tell us. I mean look, you found out we boned and didn't judge." Crew sips his coffee.

I cough.

"Okay, so you may have judged a little, but still, you can tell us and *we won't* judge you."

Hallie shuffles uncomfortably as I take a sip of my coffee.

"Or you can just stay mute," he shrugs his shoulders up, "anyway, I am going to get dressed and I'll be on my way..." Crew stands slowly, reluctantly almost, then finishes the last mouthful of his coffee. "Eat your toast, I slaved away this morning preparing that," he tips his head and winks at me and my stomach flips before he disappears into the bathroom, picking his clothes up as he does.

Me and Hallie exchange looks as I take a bite into the buttery toast, and I groan. I'm not ready for the next couple of hours.

How do you say goodbye to your best friend and keep your emotions in check?

Chapter Twenty-Three

Crew

"That's the last of it," I call out, grunting as I pick up the moving box and edge towards the steps that lead to the removal van.

"You sure? Want me to do one last sweep?" Rich asks, taking the box off me and then passing it to Will who loads it into the back of the van.

"You can do," I shrug not overly bothered as my mind is somewhere else. Cody wasn't here and I was sure she would have been here by now. *Maybe she wasn't coming.*

"Oi oi," Harry calls out as we see a taxi roll towards the kerb before stopping and Hallie and Cody step out. She looks stunning as always, wearing a long-sleeved white crop top and high-waisted jeans with trainers. Her long brown hair is in loose waves and her eyes are surrounded in dark eyeshadow which make her beautiful blue eyes stand out even more than they usually do. She smiles as she begins to walk towards me, I step closer to her, closing the gap. Her arms wrap around my neck, and I pick her up, her legs wrapping round my waist.

"Hey, baby girl," I whisper, burying my face in her hair and inhaling.

"Veto," she whispers as she tightens her grip, "what am I going to do without you?"

"You're going to keep smashing it, I won't be gone forever."

"I don't feel like you're coming back," she whispers and her lips brush against my ear, I turn my head and let my lips trace against hers.

"I promise you my little dove, I'm coming back..." I breathe and she chokes, her eyes filling with unshed tears, "just in a couple of years."

She clings to me, and I don't want to put her down. She tightens her legs around my waist.

"I want you to thrive without me, be happy, dance in the rain and I'll be home before you know it. And I'll make a promise to you..." I slowly put her down and she whimpers, "if it's raining when I return, I'm going to kiss the fuck out of you." I smirk, clasping her head in my hands.

"And what if it's not raining?" She smiles, and I see her bottom lip trembling and it breaks my heart.

"Then I'll kiss the fuck out of you anyway, pudding chops."

"Veto," she chokes out a laugh and I kiss the tip of her nose.

"Cody," I breathe, tucking a strand of hair behind her ear. Our eyes volleying back and forth with each other's. "I... I mean," I laugh, rubbing the back of my neck, the fucking nerves are suffocating me. "I just wanted..." and she stares at me with her big wide eyes waiting and hanging on every word I say.

Just tell her. Ask her to come with you, tell her you're

head over heels in love with her. It's just three words. Three, little, words.

"Cody, I..."

"Crew?" And I feel my heart fall, freezing as I lift my eyes to see Candy standing there with her suitcases, beaming at me.

Not now, for fuck's sake, what is she even doing here?!

Cody wipes a stray tear that runs down her cheek and steps away, Hallie wraps her arms round her shoulders and suddenly I feel like a heartless cunt.

"What are you doing here?" I joke, Candy throwing herself at me and smashing her lips over mine and suddenly I feel repulsed. Nausea swarms through me.

"I was always coming here, fuzzy butt," she laughs, throwing her arm down and looking over her shoulder at Cody, Hallie and the boys. Will is standing close to Hallie, Rich has his fingers locked through Cody's and my blood boils. My eyes shut as I take a moment to let my anger go.

Candy knew what she was doing, I was so close to letting those three words slip off my tongue, so close to asking Cody to come with me but Candy had to ruin it.

I push past Candy and rush for Cody, taking her hands in mine as I pull them from Rich's.

"Tell me to stay and I'll stay, tell me what you *want*, that you *want* more than this?" I practically beg, my heart thrashing in my chest, thumping against my rib cage.

She says nothing.

"Tell me to stay," I pull her for a hug so only she can hear, a lump the size of an apple lodged in my throat. "Tell me... say the words," I whisper, my eyes glassing over as I wait for her.

"Fuck you," she whispers back, "I said I would come with you, but you decided to date Candy and take her with you..." she pauses, pushing me away and I see the hurt in her eyes. "Go and live your life Crew, be happy, dance in the rain," she just about manages as a tear falls and rolls down her cheek.

"I'm coming for that promise, okay?" My voice is hoarse as my throat thickens.

She steps further away from me, swiping angry tears away as she turns and fucking walks away from me.

"Come on baby, let's go," Candy slips her hand in mine and tugs me away.

My heart hurts, my brain screams at me, and my gut feels like a knife is being twisted, but instead of following the *love of my life,* the *light of my soul* and the *key to my heart*, I walk away.

Chapter Twenty Four

Cody

Two Years Later

"Baby?" He calls out as I re-arrange the fridge with the shopping that has been delivered.

"Yeah?" I answer, closing the fridge. Smiling as he turns the corner, and his smile meets mine.

"Want to go for dinner tonight?" Julian asks as he wraps his arms around my waist, pulling me into him and placing a soft kiss on my lips.

"Could do…" I trail off, "but we've just got this food in."

"So what? We're celebrating." He nips my jaw as I tip my head back.

"We've been celebrating for six months," I push him away and tighten my ponytail.

Me and Julian have been engaged for six months. It was completely out of the blue and I wasn't expecting it. I felt a little hesitant because truthfully, he wasn't Crew, but he was very patient and understanding when I told him I needed some time. I speak to Crew every few weeks, he tells me how much he is loving his job and that him and Candy are getting on well so that makes me happy. I don't think I will ever truly be over Crew, but he was my first love. You never get over your first love. There is always a part of them that imprints on you, and it doesn't matter how much you try to get over them, they will always be there.

"Let's go out, we can get Hallie and co to meet us too."

I thought about it for the moment, and why shouldn't we? It's Friday, and after the day at work I have had I could do without cooking.

"Oh, come on then, let me just get changed." I press onto my tiptoes and kiss him on the lips.

Dressed in a casual orange summer dress and tanned wedges I make my way downstairs, clasping the back of my gold hoop in place.

"You look lovely, sweetheart," Julian kisses me on the cheek, his hand wrapping round my back and pulling me close to him, I lean into him.

Pulling up outside the restaurant, Julian pays the taxi driver and we head into *STK* to see the girls and their partners sitting there. I smile when I see Hallie and Will cuddled up, Tia is sitting with Matt and Mabel with George. It's rare that we are all out together, normally Mabel comes by herself because of George working and Matt never comes along usually, but I suppose now they've got their son they try to get all the time they can together.

"Guys, it's so great to see you all," I say as I place kisses on all their cheeks then I take my seat next to Julian.

Once dinner is had, the guys move to the bar area, and I don't know why but I can feel the tension between Will and Julian, but then again it could be my mind playing tricks on me.

"So, how's it going?" Hallie asks as she sips her vodka and cranberry through a straw.

"Yeah, it's going good," I half smile as I let my eyes wander over to Will and Julian once more.

"Why do you keep looking over there?" Mabel asks; as always, she doesn't miss a beat.

"I feel like there is some tension brewing between Will and Julian, but then maybe I am overthinking it?" I turn my head to look at the girls. Mabel rolls her eyes and Tia shakes her head from side to side and then my eyes land on Hallie, her eyes falling to her lap. "Hallie," I press, my teeth grit and my jaw locked.

"It's nothing," her guilty eyes find mine.

"Really?" I sit back, crossing my arms across my chest.

She knots her fingers.

"Please just tell me, my anxiety and over thinking mind can't take much more."

She sighs, "He just feels like Julian ruined your chances with Crew."

My eyes widen, "And why does he think that?"

"I don't know, he just thinks that you were always going to end up together," she shrugs her shoulders up, "and now with Julian in the picture that isn't going to happen."

"And so did I, Hallie. I thought we were going to end up together, but things just don't work out the way they're supposed too. Either way it isn't Julian that ruined our chances, that's all down to me and Crew, we made our choices." I bite out, reaching for my drink and take a mouthful waiting for the vodka to burn my throat.

Mabel and Tia just sit, sipping their drinks not knowing what to say. I inhale deeply, closing my eyes for a moment. I hate that I still feel so deeply for Crew, but he didn't want me. He chose Candy and that's something that I must deal with.

"How's baby Luca?" I ask Tia, smiling.

"He is great, can't believe he is nearly two. It's true what they say that you blink, and it's gone. It feels like he was a new-born only yesterday," she sighs.

"How do you think I feel! Rocco starts school this year," Mabel knocks her drink back in one hit, "I have a four-year-old," she wails.

Tensing slightly when I feel Julian's hand round the back of my neck as he squeezes it a little tighter than normal, then places a kiss on my temple. Will slides in next to Hallie and whispers something in her ear which causes her to blush.

"You ready to go home, kiddo?" Julian leans down and whispers against my skin.

I nod. I don't want to go home; I want to stay with my friends but seems like everyone is having the same idea.

We say our goodbyes and jump into the waiting taxi.

"Did you have a nice night with your friends?" Julian asks, a slight maliciousness to his tone.

"Yeah, it was nice. Thank you for arranging it." I lean into him and his hand slips between my thighs.

"You're most welcome," he leans across, trailing kisses along my cheekbone and up to the shell of my ear, "how about you give me a nice thank you when we get home by getting on your knees and blowing me," I feel his smirk against my cool skin, and he makes me shudder.

I nod, unable to speak.

The sex between me and Julian isn't great. He is more about getting head then actually having sex with me, but it all falls back to the same thing. They can't be arsed to work and get me off. I haven't had an orgasm through sex since

Crew. Julian pins my hands above my head when we fuck and takes away my chance to touch myself, the only thing that will guarantee an orgasm when I have sex and he doesn't like it. So, he gave up. He will go down on me occasionally or push me to my knees to get his dick sucked because he is fucking selfish.

I feel my anger begin to bubble as the thoughts consume me, but I manage to let it simmer, until eventually, it disappears.

I could have had Crew, but I didn't open my mouth and tell him how I felt, but then again, neither did he.

Chapter Twenty-Five

Crew

PUTTING THE DIRTY PAN IN THE SINK, I LET IT SOAK into the bubbles and dry my hands. Twisting the cap off my beer I fall into my sofa and flick through the channels. I am over being here now. I am not interested in this job like I was two years ago and that's all because of Cody. I shouldn't have just walked away. I let Candy in, I should have told her to go back home. I didn't invite her to go with me, the last we agreed was I was to let her know what I wanted but she turned up anyway. Put me on the spot and Cody spooked.

I take a sip of my beer, drinking a quarter of the bottle down. And now she was with that fucking douche Julian and it makes me so angry. The thought that he is touching and kissing what I want. What I have always wanted.

The apartment is silent, and I hate it. I never minded living alone back in London but here, I fucking hate it. The boys still come up once a month, but Cody hasn't been up since her and Julian made their relationship official, and I miss her. I text her every few weeks letting her know that I am fine and happy with my life here with Candy, but little does she know that I am miserable as sin and Candy left a year ago. She could see I wasn't over Cody, I never lied to her. I told her that Cody was the love of my life, but she was the one that got away. After a while of her loving me, with me not loving her back she moved back home. I couldn't blame her, I agreed with her choices because she deserved to be loved by someone that loved her back.

And so did I.

Will has been filling me in on *sir douche a lot.* He doesn't trust him, which makes me not trust him because Will trusts everyone. I'm festering, lost in my own thoughts and it is driving me insane. Turning my head, I see my resignation letter sitting on the side table. I have been toying with the idea of leaving my post and heading back home for my noise complaints and speeding tickets. I was happy. I had the best partner, and I was close to my friends. Here, I have no one. I say *hi* to the men and women in the station but they're not my friends.

I needed to sleep on my decision. It was a pay cut and also a waste of the last two years that I have put blood, sweat and tears into this promotion.

I've already floated it past the guys, and they want me back, more so to try and get Cody away from the douche canoe, but I couldn't do it to her if she was happy. I only wanted her to be happy. That's all I have ever wanted since meeting her and if her happiness was with Julian then I needed to swallow the bitter pill and let it go.

Even if my heart didn't want to.

Chapter Twenty-Six

Cody

Rushing out of my florist, I had ten minutes to get to Kensington for my final dress appointment. Julian had pushed for us to get married in the October and although it felt a little rushed, I was also excited when we set the date. Locking up behind me I turned and practically run down the street, Julian would be furious if I miss this fitting. Standing at the pedestrian crossing I continued pressing the button, praying that it would turn green any second.

"Come on, come on," I pleaded. As soon as it turned green, I power marched over the busy crossing when I bumped shoulders with someone. *Shit.*

"Oh my god, I am so sorry." I said to the lady that had dropped her shopping all over the road. I bent down and grabbed a can of beans when her head snapped up and her eyes met my gaze. My heart plummeted deep into my chest as her eyes widened.

"Candy?" I exclaim, my voice high pitched.

"Cody," she breathes as she backs up onto her knees, ignoring her shopping that is disregarded all over the floor.

"What are you doing here? Are you and Crew visiting for the weekend?"

I see her face fall, before she then scurries to pick her bits up off the floor.

"Candy?" My voice is a little sterner now as I stand, still holding the can of beans.

"We're not together," she rushes out and avoids eye contact. "We haven't been together in over a year..." she stops and finally looks at me and she sees my face fall when it hits me that Crew never told me.

"He never told you," she breathes, rolling her lips and the sting behind my eyes feels like a thousand needles. I shake my head from side to side because I can't muster the words. "I'm sorry, but I truly believe he didn't say anything because you're happy," she smiles softly, her hand reaching out for me and rubbing the top of my arm. "I see congratulations are in order," her eyes move to my left hand, and I nod.

A car horn blasts and we're both blasted out of our trance, the rest of the world moving quickly around us whilst we're standing frozen in time.

She holds her hands up and begins to walk off, "Take care Cody, best of luck in your marriage."

"Bye Candy," I whisper back but she is already gone.

STANDING ON THE SMALL PODIUM, I STARE IN THE mirror as the seamstress helps me into my dress. Sliding it up my hips I slip my arms into my straps. I say straps, they're little laced cuffs that sit just off my shoulders. I have a beaded lace bodice in a sweetheart neckline and the skirt just flows in tulle away from my waist. I wanted something simple and pretty and this dress is just that.

"Cody," the seamstress snaps her fingers in front of my eyes and I come round, apologising. Truth is, my mind is elsewhere.

"Sorry, so sorry," I whisper as I skim my hands down the material of my dress.

"It's okay, in dreamland with your soon to be husband?" She winks, and I nod. *Oh, if only you knew*.

"Yes, yes," I fake a laugh as I stare at the woman in the reflection. This is all I have ever wanted. To be married. To be loved. But not like this. I feel heartbroken and like I have lost the love of my life even though I never had him in the first place.

"Well Cody, I must say you are going to make the most beautiful bride in eight weeks," she beams, standing like a proud mum. A pang shot through me, maybe I should have had my mum here for my final fitting, but I wanted a private moment to myself.

I smile and thank her before she begins to undo the dress for me. Once I was undressed, I stare at myself in the mirror, the marks and bruises that were once prominent seem to be fading as the days go on. Julian wasn't silly. He knew that when he marked me, he would do it where no one would see.

Ever since the night out a few months ago with all of my friends, something in Julian changed. His moods were up and down, he was out working later and later and when he was at home, he was horrible. I couldn't think for myself most of the time and now I am a nervous wreck whenever I don't do as he asks. His demands are getting more intense and so is his abuse, but I stay because I am trapped, too frightened of what he would do if I walked away.

No one is going to save me; I just have to live with the

consequences and my poor choices. I sigh, pulling my top over my head before fastening the button up on my trousers.

Will was right to not like or trust Julian. But I would never admit that. Not to anyone.

SITTING AT MY MUM'S IN MY LOUNGE WEAR, I SIP A beer while my dad watches F1 on the TV. After my dress fitting, I went home to freshen up and slip into something a little more comfortable. Julian was working late tonight, and the girls were all at home. Normally it was only Monday nights which meant going to my parents for dinner, but I didn't fancy sitting at home alone tonight. I felt needy and clingy and if Julian wasn't here for me then I fell back on my parents.

Sighing, I scroll through my phone aimlessly. Julian's work schedule was becoming more and more in the last couple of months, he said it was to pay for the wedding, but I don't believe him. My dad is footing most of the bill, Julian is only covering his suits and the drinks. I never wanted a big wedding but here we are, having a forty-thousand-pound wedding for one day. I wanted to elope to Gretna Green and just marry someone because they're all I care about, not the big fancy day that goes with it. Is it wrong that I am secretly hoping Julian is having an affair so I can leave him? Would he let me leave? Or would he hold me prisoner in my own home because he is a narcissistic bastard? I was weak. I could just call the police, but what would they say? Julian would charm them and tell them that I was making it up for attention. I know how he works, then I would get lost in the system until I am beaten to death.

"You okay pumpkin?" My dad asks as he pulls his eyes away from the TV as *Verstappen* pushes into pole position, pulling me from my own, dark and morbid thoughts.

"Yeah, I'm fine," I lie, taking another sip of beer.

"You sure? You just seem quiet, a little distracted..."

I nod, "Honestly, I am fine. Just tired," I shrug my shoulders up and I turn my attention to the television, my dad notes my mood and faces forward.

We sit in silence until my mum walks in the room with sandwiches and cakes. She places them down on the table and then disappears and re-appears with two bowls of crisps.

"This is not good for my wedding diet," I smirk, reaching for an egg mayonnaise and cress sandwich.

"You don't need to diet," she tsks, rolling her eyes as she picks up ham and mustard. She has done a little afternoon tea style spread for us.

"I bumped into Crew's mother the other day," she says over the roaring of the television, dad is sitting on the edge of his seat as *Sainz* and *Verstappen* are chasing for the finish line.

"Oh, did you," I say, trying my best to sound uninterested.

"Mmhmm," she nods, reaching for a salted crisp, "he is coming back apparently." And instantly my blood runs cold, my heart pumps in my chest.

"Really?" I sit forward as my dad reaches for a beef and horseradish sandwich.

"Apparently so," she says nonchalantly as she takes another bite of her sandwich.

"Interesting," I chirp, trying to ignore the ball of anxiety that keeps growing in my stomach, *he's coming home?*

"Did he RSVP to the wedding?" Shuffling forward she

171

pops a crisp into her mouth then pinches up a salmon and cream cheese sandwich. *Damn, she really went all out with the sandwiches.*

I picked up a cream cheese and cucumber sandwich, I promise, we're not this posh. I have no idea why she chose this filling.

"He didn't," I shake my head and take a bite as I reach for my beer.

"Don't you want a glass of wine with me?" My mum frowns as she eyes my beer bottle.

"That depends mother, is it going to taste like rancid cat piss, or did you spend more than five pound on a bottle?"

She over exaggerates and rolls her eyes.

"I'll have you know I picked up a lovely bottle of Provence from the wine shop round the corner, would you like some miss snobby?"

I laugh out loud, "Please, that would be *delightful.*"

I DECIDED TO WALK HOME, THE SUMMER BREEZE WAS warm on my skin. I was wearing a tee and converse. Julian messaged and told me he was on his way home. He can get a little funny if I'm not home by the time he is. I seem to give in to his beck and calls and I don't like it. I'm not that girl yet here I am, running home like a good puppy dog to be there waiting for him. I actually make myself a little sick.

I stop in my tracks as my mind wanders to Crew. I can't believe he is coming home. Our conversations had fizzled out, but I wasn't sure why. My fingers hovered over his name too many times since running into Candy but I decided against it. If he wanted me to know he wasn't with her anymore he surely would have told me. We were closer than that. *Or so you thought*. My subconscious gently reminds me.

Sighing, I drag my feet along the pavement suddenly feeling solemn. I can't remember the last time that I felt this low. Normally I have a day or so and then I get over it. But this feels deeper than my normal episode. I decide to walk the long way home, Julian will just have to wait, I'll deal with the consequences of my actions. After the news today I needed to clear my head before I went home. Julian would read it all over my face. I wasn't a good liar. I didn't have a good poker face. Julian would sniff it out of me and after witnessing what he gets like over the smallest thing, fear cripples me at the thoughts of what he would do when I've made him angry.

I walk past the shop and take a moment, smiling. Renovations have begun, I managed to get the space next door which I didn't think would happen. It had been up for sale for ages and I finally talked them round. She was reluctant to sell because it was her late husband's and even though it was up for sale, she didn't really want to let it go.

I got it.

I don't think I would want to lose something that was once belonged to the man I loved. Thinking at how the space is going to open the café area up, there is going to be a beautiful library with a small hooked, sliding ladder on the floor to ceiling bookshelves. *Beauty and the beast eat your heart out*. Eventually I would like to do book themed afternoon tea, based on all of my favourite books. I sigh blissfully. This is a dream I have had for a while and I cannot wait to see it come to life. Julian *was* fantastic with helping me organise the space but decided he didn't want to do the fit out, something about schedules clashing. But it was fine.

You don't mix business with pleasure. He wanted to over-look the works that were being carried out, but from a distance but he is no longer interested in doing that. So it's just me.

I was so lucky to be in a fortunate place when Luna and Taron put this shop on the market, I know it was a hard sale for her but she had twins and another baby on the way. I struggle some days and it's just me so how she managed with kids in tow I will never know.

I nod to myself and turn to make my way home, I don't live far from the shop and I like that I can just walk to it and to my parent's place if I fancy it.

Pulling my earphones out of my bag, I push them into my ear and press play on *Taylor Swift – You Are In Love* and I swoon. Losing myself in the music, singing along when I see a car flashing its headlights at me. I still, panic bolting through me as the music continues to play. As the car gets closer, I breathe out a breath of relief. It's Julian.

Stepping forward, my legs take me towards the car. He pulls kerbside, leaves the engine running and exits the car. His brows are furrowed, his jaw tight as he storms over to me.

"Where were you?" He snaps, his eyes bloodshot. He reached out, grabbing the top of my arm with force.

"Walking home," I half laugh and try to tug my arm from his grip. My eyes widened and I began to panic as I tug again, but his vice like grip is too much. He has never hurt me in public before.

"Were you sniffing around Crew? Heard he is back in town," he grits out, pulling me towards him. His breath is rancid, I can smell the alcohol and it makes me dry heave.

"No! I've been at my mum and dad's; you know I have!" I snap, tugging again but he only tightens his grip. "Ouch,

Julian, you're hurting me," I whine, tears pricking my eyes. His breaths are ragged like a bull as he snorts out his nose. He wipes his mouth, licking his lips and smirking. He looks over his shoulder, his grip loosening slightly, and I tug but he is too quick for me.

"Please just let me go," I whisper, begging.

"Shut up!" He barks, slapping me across the cheek with the back of his hand and fuck did it burn. Tears prick my eyes, a burning lump in my throat as my head snaps to the side, a whoosh of air leaving my lungs from the contact.

"Shit, Cody, I'm sorry." Julian panders to me, grabbing my face and turning me to face him. His eyes volley back and forth between mine. I choke out sobs, but I manage to shove him off me.

I hear his footsteps beat on the pavement behind me and Julian's fingers wrap around my wrist. He pulls me back into him, "Get in the car, let me take you home," he begs, and I am too scared to say no. I am trembling on the inside.

I nod, numbness filling me as I stalk towards the car. He opens the door, letting me in and closing it behind me. Tears sit heavy, I am afraid to blink because as soon as I do the tears are going to fall.

The driver's door slams and I jump in my seat. I daren't look at him. He pushes the car into first gear and pulls away, wheel spinning as he does. Bracing myself, I push my hands onto the dashboard of the car.

"I'm sorry." I feel his penetrative stare burning into the side of my head. "I just get so wound up with that fucking idiot Crew, he is coming back to steal you. I knew he liked you, fuck, he probably wanted to *fuck* you," he snarls.

I stay mute. Julian is like a mad man, why the hell did I

get in this car. He swerves round the corner and I swear we ended up on two wheels.

"Say something!" He bellows, smashing his hand on the steering wheel as anger seeps through him again. I shake, bile rising in my throat as he takes his eyes off the road and hurls lashing after lashings of abusive words towards me. Tears roll down my cheeks, hot, burning tears and my throat aches, the lump in my throat bobbing up and down, choking me.

I look in the side mirror and see blue flashing lights and relief sweeps over me. *I'm safe.*

"Fuck!!" He screams, his hand smashing down on the steering wheel again. I have no idea what's happened to get him so drunk and abusive tonight. Was it work? Or is it really Crew? I have *never* seen him like this.

The siren wails and Julian pulls over reluctantly.

"Keep your fucking mouth shut," he snaps, and I nod, nibbling on the bottom of my lip. Pulling down the sun visor, I slide the cover across and look in the small mirror. Running my ring fingers under my eyes and trying to clear the smudged mascara. I turn my head to the left and see the redness growing along my cheekbone. It throbs. I need ice.

The police car stops, its blue lights still flashing when I see a police officer approach the driver's side. My heart is thumping so fast in my chest making me feel nauseous. Closing my eyes, I am praying that Julian fucks up and I'll be okay.

I hear a tap on the glass and it startles me. My nerves are shot.

"Button it," he snaps.

He pushes the window button and it slides down.

"Good evening officer, is everything okay?" Julian plays

it cool, but there's no way the officer can't smell the alcohol. The car stinks.

I see the officer bend down to look inside the car and that's when our eyes meet.

Crew.

Chapter Twenty-Seven

Crew

I GROAN AS I DRIVE ROUND THE CORNER; I AM READY TO go home. It's been a day. It's just gone eleven fifteen and I am off shift in fifteen minutes. *Fifteen minutes to get through.*

Tightening my grip round the steering wheel, I sit up when I see a reckless blue *BMW* speeding and swerving through the lanes.

Picking up the radio, I call it in.

"So close yet so far," I grumble and flick the sirens on. The driver hits the brakes, then seems to pick up speed again before giving in and pulling over.

The sirens wail through the summer night as I pull behind them, leaving the engine running, I step from the car and slowly and cautiously walk towards the pulled over vehicle. My shoes pound the pavement and my skin tingles. Standing at the side of the car, I knock on the window with my curled index finger three times. It slides down and the smell of booze hits me in the face. *Jesus.*

I sigh, leaning down to look through the window and I

swear the air is knocked from my lungs when I see who is sitting in the passenger side. *Cody.*

A trembling mess, make-up staining her face and her eyes are pinned to me.

"Can I ask you to step out the vehicle?" I order, gritting my teeth and clenching my jaw.

"Can I ask why?"

Prick.

"Just get out the car." My tone is sterner now.

Julian's head snaps to the side as he silently speaks to Cody. She whimpers then turns to look out the window.

Stepping back from the car, Julian opens the door and stumbles out. As soon as he is out of the car, I grab him and push him on the bonnet and swiftly cuff him.

Julian struggles and I push him back down.

"Stay down!" I shout and thankfully, Julian listens. I wait a moment before I rush round to her side and open the door.

"Petal," I breathe out, brushing her hair that is stuck to her skin and mixed with her tears. I suck in a breath when I see her red and bruising cheek.

"Did that *cunt* do that to you?" My anger has reached boiling point. She chokes on a sob, her hands trembling. Leaning over her, I unplug her and pull her into my arms. I let her cry, her whole body shakes in my embrace.

"It's okay, I've got you, I've got you..." I whisper, reassuring her. How the fuck did I miss this?

Chapter Twenty-Eight

Cody

I STRETCH AND WAKE, MY EYES TAKING A MOMENT TO adjust to my surroundings. Rubbing my eyes, I wince and suddenly the flashbacks from last night haunt me. Sitting up, I grab my phone and see missed calls and messages from the girls. Pressing my hand to my head, I open the messages and quickly scroll through them. I can't decipher any of them. My head and cheek are throbbing. Throwing back the covers, I pad across the floor when the bedroom door swings open and I see Crew. My heart sings in my chest being close to him, but fear and anxiety cripples me.

"Morning twinkle, how are you feeling?"

I realise I have been holding in my breath. "Veto."

"There's my girl," he smiles as he closes the gap between us and hands me a coffee then drops two painkillers into my hand. "Take them, drink up and get back into bed," he winks, "that's an order."

I smile, my steps faltering back as I sit in bed and swallow down the painkillers with a mouthful of coffee. A deep, heavy sigh rocks through me as I stare at him. He looks wounded and lost.

"I heard you were coming back; I didn't know you *were* back." And that's when I feel the anger surge through me.

He shrugs his shoulders up, his boyish grin spreading on his face. "Well, I thought it would be a nice surprise." He backs up, "Obviously under different circumstances."

I nod, grinding my back teeth down.

"I'm going to get you a cool compress for your face. Be back soon." And with that, he disappears. I close my eyes and steady my breathing, I need to cool it. I am angry with Crew, but I am disappointed in myself for getting myself in this situation.

Placing my coffee cup on the side, I reach for the water and down it. I felt thirsty suddenly. Popping it back I let myself fall into my pillows. I felt exhausted.

Scrolling through my phone, I find Hallie's name and press dial. She answers instantly.

"Cody!? Are you okay?" the panic evident in her voice.

"Yeah, I'm fine. I promise."

"That monster, Will was fucking right." Hallie snaps and I smooth my finger and thumb over my brows.

"Hallie, please," my voice is quiet as I try to reason with her.

"*What* Cody? He hit you, picked you up drunk and then drove like a lunatic. It's lucky that Crew was there! What if he wasn't? What if he drove you into a ditch and killed you!"

"I know," I agree with her, but then find myself defending him. "He has never done anything like that before. It was out of character for him; he loves me, I know he loves me."

"Can you hear yourself right now?" She barks, I can hear Will's muffled shouts in the background. And yes, I could hear myself and I wanted to step out of my body and physically shake me.

"It's not that simple, we're engaged, I can't just leave him."

"And what?! Call the engagement off. Jesus, Cody. If I could walk away from a marriage after so many years, you can walk away from an abusive monster you're engaged to." Her tone is harsh and then I'm hit with silence. She cut me off.

Crew walks through the door just at that moment and my heart sinks. Did he hear? Of course, he did. The walls are thin in this house and he only went down to get ice.

"Here," his voice is soft as he scoots towards me on the bed. Placing the ice on my cheek, I wince then lean into him.

Seconds that feel like minutes pass before either one of us says anything.

"Julian was held last night. They breathalysed him, and he was three times over the legal limit. I'm not sure what working late means to him but drinking that amount at work is wrong in itself. Let alone driving to you, hitting you and then driving home. He is going to be charged Cody, with driving whilst under the influence and actual bodily harm." Crew's tone is firm and matter of fact. I don't think I have ever seen him this serious. "You're not going back to him, are you?"

His eyes burn into mine and I can feel the disappointment filling the room at my silence. I let my eyes fall to my lap.

"Please Cody, don't be so reckless and foolish," his voice is a plea, his large hand reaching forward and taking mine in his.

"It's not that simple..." I want to look at him, fuck the

pull is so intense but I can't. Because everything he is saying is true, and if I give in and look him in the eyes, I will say anything to make him happy.

"It is! Jesus, Cody." He snatches his hand from mine and rakes his fingers through his hair, "Don't become this girl, you're so much better than that," the desperation in his voice splinters through me.

"Am I?" I question and finally, my eyes meet his.

"Yes," he breathes, shuffling closer to me and cupping my cheek. "You are."

And there it is.

The tingling of my skin as it pebbles. My body shivering under his touch, my skin erupting into goosebumps and the hairs standing on the back of my neck, all while my heart races in my chest, beating along to the song that has only ever beat for him.

CREW HAS STAYED BY MY SIDE ALL DAY. WE HAVEN'T spoken about Julian or what happened anymore. I need time to think about it, he *hurt* me, physically and emotionally. I've had a long soak in the bath, and I have had a cry whilst listening to *Celine Dion – all by myself.*

Hallie has messaged a couple of times; I know she would be beating herself up for the way we left things. Mabel and Tia have been amazing as well.

Sitting on the edge of my bed, I feel numb. Everything hitting me and getting consumed by mixed emotions, I wanted to cry but I didn't have any more tears left to cry. The lump and the burn in my throat were there, but nothing else. Wrapped in a towel, my dark hair was dripping down my back and my fringe was parted in two as water ran down my face. Staring in front of me, I couldn't avert my gaze, even if I wanted to. I felt the bed dip, my hair being pulled from my face before a brush was dragged through the knots.

"I've got you," his voice was soft, as he brushed from the root, down the crown of my head and down to the ends. That's when the tears decided to fall again.

Chapter Twenty-Nine

Crew

I BRUSHED HER HAIR, I CARED FOR HER AND GOT HER dressed into her pyjamas and I walked her downstairs to the lounge. She hadn't spoken. She hadn't eaten and I was worried. Edging towards the kitchen, I pull my phone out my pocket and call Will.

"Yo, you okay?" He said as I hear Maverick squealing in the background.

"Yeah," I say quietly, leaning back and looking round the door frame at an absent Cody. "Is Hallie there?"

"Yeah yeah, she is just bathing Maverick."

"Okay," I flick the kettle on and drum my fingers on the worktop as I wait.

"Baby, fuzzy butt is on the phone," he bellows.

"You arsehole," I grit as the kettle clicks. Throwing a tea bag into two mugs I cover them with boiling water then add the milk. Scooping a sugar up, I stir it in then strain the tea bag and dropping it into the caddy on the side.

"Hey, fuzzy, all okay?" Hallie says, chirpy.

"Please, stop with the name."

She chuckles, "What can I do for you *handsome?*"

"Okay, that name can stay," I snort, "I need help, I don't know what to do..." my voice breaks and I step back to see if she's moved. She hasn't. Sighing.

"What's she doing?" Her tone changes.

"Sitting on the sofa just staring, she had a bath, she's cried to Celine Dion and then I walked in the bedroom to find her sitting on the edge of the bed with water dripping down her face from her sodden wet hair."

Hallie sucks in a breath.

"I brushed it out, got her dressed and led her to the living room. She hasn't moved since. Thought I should make her a cup of tea."

"Keep doing what you're doing, I'll be over in ten."

"Thank you, Hallie."

"No, thank you Crew."

Hanging the phone up I place it face down on the worktop and grabbed the mugs.

"Hey baby, drink this." My voice is soft as I hand it to her. Her glassy eyes meet mine and she smiles.

"Thank you," her voice wavers.

"What's on your mind? Tell me..." I push as I sit down next to her.

She turns, her hands trembling, tears threatening to leave her beautiful eyes.

"You fucking left me," her voice cracks as the emotion is thick. My heart sinks into my stomach.

"I'm sorry sweetness..." but I don't get a chance to continue, her eyes widen, her nostrils flare as her breaths become heavier.

"You don't get to call me *sweetness,* you don't get to do that anymore. I'm not your baby, not your *little dove.* You lost that right when *you left me*! You left me!" She screams, hot tears rolling down her cheeks. "You went and started a new life with *her,* you fucking left me when I needed you," she chokes on her sobs, her face screwing up and turning away from me and my heart breaks.

"Cody..." I say softly, reaching my hand forward to move her hair from her face but she pulls away, her head snapping round and the anger that was once plastered all over her beautiful face has been replaced with sadness. I stand from the sofa, "I'm just going to make a few calls," I lie, but I need to give her some space.

"What if he comes back for me?" She whispers a short while later when I sit back down next to her. The fear is etched over her face, her chest rises fast as the panic sears through her.

"Baby..." I stammer, "Cody," I edge closer to her, but my voice is hesitant. I place my tea on the coffee table, "I promise, he isn't coming back." I reach my hand out to brush my thumb pad across her cheek so I can wipe the stray tear that is rolling down her cheek, but she stills, slapping my hand away before I can even touch her.

"But how do you know?" She chokes, her body shakes and my heart breaks. Her shoulders fall and all I want to do is pull her into an embrace. But I don't.

"Because that cunt isn't making bail baby, he isn't going to be walking the streets for a while and by the time he is, we will be moved far, far away."

Her beautiful blue eyes are rimmed with tears, her teeth sinking into her bottom lip. I feel my insides burn, my cock hardening.

"Cody..." I whisper, standing up. I know that look. She rushes towards me, her lips crashing into mine. I should pull away, but I don't want to. I've wanted this moment for the last two years and now I finally have her, I don't want to stop.

Running my hands under her, I lift her effortlessly as her legs wrap around my waist. I walk her over to the other side of the living room, a shudder of breath leaving her as her back hits the wall.

"Baby," I whisper, my lips breaking away from hers as I trail them down her jawline, her neck, her collar bone. My erection is pushing into her through the material that is acting as a barrier between us. She rotates her hips, grinding her sweet as fuck pussy over my hardened cock.

"Please," she begs and the tears fall, I drag my lips back over her pebbled skin until my lips are back over hers, our tongues swirling and dancing with each other's. "I need this, Crew... I haven't felt *like this* in so long, I need this," she breathes out in a moan, but in that moment we're interrupted by her doorbell.

She jumps, pushing away from me, her feet hitting the floor, her cheeks a crimson red.

"It's just Hallie, angel."

I step up and move towards the door, giving it a second as I re-adjust myself. Pulling the catch off and opening the door to see Hallie with a bag full of shit.

"Hey," she sings, dropping the bag on the floor and I hear clinks.

"Wine? Really?"

"Trust me Crew, you may think you know her, but you don't *know* her like I do," she shrugs her shoulders up, "this isn't my first rodeo when it comes to Cody."

"She is an emotional wreck; she is traumatised, and you

think wine is going to help?" I push my hand through my hair.

"Watch and learn fuzzy butt, watch and learn."

I clench my fists, tip my head back and breathe. *Trust the process.*

Chapter Thirty

Cody

"Whyyyyyyy?" I groan, swaying in my seat as I spill the wine from my glass all over myself, "Why do I always end up with the dickheads?" I pout and stick my bottom lip out, my eyes crossing as I try to look down my nose.

"You don't always end up with dickheads, look at Crew," Hallie smirks and eyes Crew. He rolls his eyes.

"Crew is an exception," I sulk, sitting back and taking a sip of wine only to be met with disappointment that it's empty.

"Let me go top you up," Hallie smirks and waltzes to the kitchen.

I let my head drop forward, placing my head in my hand.

"You okay?" The sofa dipped as Crew sat next to me.

"Not really, but I'll be okay," I sniffled, lifting my head to look at him. Brushing my hair out my face, his knuckles brush past my temple and across my bruised cheek.

"At least the mark has gone," he offers me a sad smile.

I nod. "Hurts like a bitch though," I shrug and let out a soft laugh, "I'm not ready to forgive you yet."

"It will petal, couple more days and it'll soothe." His voice is barely audible when he picks my hand up and places a kiss on the back of it. "And that's okay, I'm not going anywhere. I'll spend the rest of my life making it up to you."

My heart skips a beat.

"I don't deserve you," I whisper.

"Darling, you deserve all of me."

I jump back when Hallie walks in with a glass full of wine, her eyes narrowing on me and Crew.

"Was I interrupting something?" She asks, placing the glass on the coffee table and I shake my head.

"Maybe," Crew smirks, "maybe not."

"Twat," she taps him round the back of the head in a playful manner. He laughs, rubbing the back of his head. Stepping back, she grabs her cross-body bag off the sofa and places it over her head.

"Right, I've got to go. Cody," her eyes meet mine, her facial features softening somehow, "are you going to be okay?"

I nod, "Yeah," my eyes move to Crew, "I am."

"Okay, if you need anything, you call me, okay?" And I don't know if she is talking to me or Crew but we both nod in agreement.

Hallie smiles, turning and heads towards the hallway that leads to the door. "Oh, and you two..." her eyes pin to both of us and my blood rushes through my veins as electricity sparks through me, "try and keep your hands off each other." And with that, she winks, smirks and walks out the door.

We sit in comfortable silence as we watch re-runs of *friends* for a while.

"What character do you think you're most like?" Crew asked as his arms rest above the top of the sofa.

"Hmmm, I don't know," I shrug, "I would say I am a mix of all of them," I turn to face him, he is already looking at me. "How about you?"

"Chandler and Joey. More so Chandler, but a little bit of Joey," he smiles, his arm that was resting on the back of the sofa edges closer to me. His callous fingertips glide across the base of my neck, tracing small circles. "Do you want anything? Tea, coffee, wine? Or would you like food?" He stills for a moment as he waits.

"No thank you," I decline politely. I see a boyish glint flash in his eyes, his lips curling into a smile.

"How about an orgasm?" He licks his lips slowly.

I snort, laughing loud and cover my mouth and nose at the humiliation of what sound just left me, he laughs along with me, holding his belly.

Seriousness blankets us for a moment and I reach for the glass that Hallie filled up, taking a sip to coat my suddenly dry mouth.

"Serious chat for a moment," I clear my throat, I don't know why but I am feeling awkward. I have no reason to; Crew has never made me feel awkward before.

Until now.

"Serious chat," his brow pings up, he leans forward, tucking his leg under himself as he shuffles back on the sofa and makes himself comfortable.

"Yes, serious." I take a big swig then place my glass down. I pick the skin round my nails.

"I haven't had an orgasm during sex since..." My cheeks blush and I feel my whole body warm with embarrassment.

"Since…" Crew's head tips forward as he looks up at me through his lashes.

"Since our night together," I spit out in a mumbled rush hoping he didn't hear me, I cover my face with my hands as I feel the heat swarm to my cheeks. I'm not hiding long when Crew wraps his fingers round my wrist and pulls them away, his eyes meeting mine.

"You haven't had an orgasm since *then!?*" He couldn't even hide the judgemental tone even if he wanted to. "Oh baby, what the fuck was he doing?" He sits up straight, rigid even, and his jaw tightens, "Don't answer that."

I ignore him and continue; I was feeling brave… but it was because of the wine.

"He never let me use my hands, used to pin them above my head so I couldn't touch myself. In the end, he gave up. Used to just make me… yano, give him head."

"Jesus Christ, what a selfish prick," he runs his hand along his dark stubble, the noise awakening something inside of me.

"Yup," I sighed, my nipples hardening at the memories of what he done to me that one night. "I even got my little bud pierced to try and make me a little more sensitive… to try and get things moving…" I don't let my eyes trail away like they want to, I keep them on him so I can see the look on his face. It doesn't disappoint. His mouth opens slowly, his jaw relaxing as his eyes widen before darkening as they narrow on me.

"I think we need to do something about your little… *situation…*" his voice is a low grumble that vibrates through me. I press my thighs together to stop the ache.

"We shouldn't," I whisper.

"I know, but I can't help it my little dove. You've just let this pent up, caged animal out of its cage. I'm hungry.

Famished. *Fucking starved.* And I need to eat, no, sorry – I need to *feast* on you. Your body needs a release, you need the endorphins to flood through your veins, a quick fix to an everlasting addiction."

"Crew," I breathe, clearly flustered as my chest rises up and down, rising faster with each breath I take.

"Cody," he closes the gap between us, running his thumb pad across my bottom lip and drags it down. "Fuck, I want to bite that lip," growling, he tugs on it then drops it just as quick.

He stands, holding his hand out for me to take. I falter, my anxiety slowly creeping up and letting its bony fingers dig into my back is they try to claw me back down.

"It's okay, it's all about *you.* As of last night, you're single."

My brows furrow, my heartbeat spiking.

"Because, petal, he will *never* have you in his life again. I will *never* let him near you. It's over for him. It's over for you. For tonight..." he stops as my hand slowly moves towards his, "you're mine."

Chapter Thirty-One

Crew

Pushing her gently to the bed, she sits, wide doe eyes penetrating mine.

"I'll be back in five, I just need to get something," I wink, stepping back and moving away from the bed. Once out of the room, I smirk and fly down the stairs and out to my car. Butterflies swarm my stomach, my skin tingles in anticipation of spending the night with her. I meant what I said earlier, I am not letting her go again. I done it once, twice, fuck, maybe even three times but I'm not doing it again. She belongs with me.

Unlocking my police car, I reach into the boot to find my kit. This should have gone back but after radioing in and letting them know it was Cody and I wasn't leaving her side they were okay with me keeping the car. Rummaging around I found the two things I was looking for. Holding them in my hands, I smirked as my eyes fell to the objects and excitement coursed through me.

Slamming the boot and locking the car, I ran back towards her house. Anticipation killing me at what was about to happen. And she had no idea the realms of pleasure I was about to take her to.

Slipping the chain across the front door, I then locked it. Hallie had already gate crashed my time with her, I wasn't about to let anyone else in. Filling two glass with water, I climbed the stairs to see Cody still sitting on the bed where I told her to.

Striding past her, I place the glasses on the bedside unit, the whole time her eyes following me round the room. Once back in front of her, I bend down slightly so our eyes are level and push her thighs apart. She is wearing a silk cami top and shorts and looks divine as per usual.

"You ready to be worshipped like the queen you are?" My lips brush against her cheek before planting a soft kiss there.

Placing a hand on the centre of her chest, I push her back. My hands place either side of her head, my lips lower over her parted ones and I dip my tongue inside as she kisses me with passion. Our kiss is raw, it's heavy and messy and my heart is lingering on for anything I can get from her. The moans that leave her lips, vibrating through me to my very core. My dick was hard and throbbing, but I had to ignore the want and need. Tonight, was about her.

"Up the bed flower."

"Veto," she smirks and fuck, she's so god damn beautiful. Shuffling up towards her wooden headboard, I lay her down.

"Don't move," I whisper, pressing my lips against hers and giving her a light kiss before pushing off the bed and walking out the bedroom. I don't know why this thought only just occurred to me, but now it's in my head, I couldn't stop until I done it.

Opening the kitchen drawer, I grab a sharp knife and

head back towards the room. Cody's eyes widen when she sees the knife and I lick my lips.

"Relax sweetheart, it isn't how it looks..." climbing onto the bed, I kneel and lean over her as I carve *CM* into the bed post and fall back onto my knees, smiling. "What did you think I was going to do? Carve my initials into your skin?" I laugh.

"I thought you were going to try some kinky fuckery shit."

"Kinky fuckery shit," I laugh loud, dropping my head back, "Oh, sweet cheeks, I'm going to kinky fuckery shit you alright, just not with a knife," I shake my head from side to side.

I place the knife on the bedside unit, pushing it away from the edge and reach for the handcuffs that I dropped at the end of the bed. Her eyes widen and light up with excitement, thrill coursing through them.

"Take your clothes off," I purr, "I want to watch you undress. But leave your panties on, I wanna be the one to remove them."

She licks her lips, sitting up and lifting her silk cami top over her head. Sinking my teeth into my bottom lip to resist the urge of locking my mouth around her pert nipples and sucking them. I palm myself through my trousers, fuck. She pulls her shorts down her legs and reveals a lacy thong.

Kneeling up, I lean across and pin her hands above her head, and cuff her to the headboard.

"Crew, I," she whimpers, "I won't be able to come without my hands."

"Do you trust me?" I ask, my fingers still wrapped round her wrists. She nods, her eyes pinned to mine as I feel her boring into my soul. "Then trust me," I breathe, our eyes locked for, a moment before I finally break the gaze.

My lips press to her neck, slowly trailing to her collar bone before I place a kiss just above each of her nipples. I move down her sternum and glide towards her belly. I look up at her through my lashes, her ice blues are on me and only me. Continuing, I nip at her sensitive skin through her thong then bury my nose inside her folds and inhale. Smirking, I feel the ring of her clit piercing rubbing against my skin. I am rock hard. Sinking my teeth into the band of her thong, I pull it away from her using only my teeth then wrap my fingers in the flimsy material and rip them in two.

"Oh," her voice is breathless. Sucking in a breath I take a moment to admire her.

"Well, that's the prettiest fucking pussy I have ever seen," and it's the truth. Her plump, pink pussy is already beginning to glisten from just my small amount of contact.

"Crew," she is practically begging, her body writhing.

"Don't move too much, pretty girl, the cuffs will nip at your beautiful skin."

My fingertips run over her sensitive skin, following an invisible map that only I can see. That only I can follow.

My fingers finally get to the one place they've been craving, the one place I have been begging to feel and be inside of again.

Gliding two fingers through her slick folds, I tease them at her opening and push them into her pussy while my thumb grazes over her clit, a gasp leaving her. I curl my fingers and rub against her spot, slowly trying to work her the way I remember.

"I just cannot get my head round the fact that that poor excuse of a man didn't spend his time on you," I growl, my temper rising at the thought of her being with someone else other than me, but that would make me a hypocrite because I was with someone else too.

Her eyes flutter closed as I continue pumping her tight cunt with my fingers. My thumb brushes in circular movements over her swollen clit, making sure I press a little harder when I near her jewellery. Her leg quivers and I can feel her walls clenching, the delicious squelch indicating that she is ready. Slipping my fingers out, I suck them clean.

"Look how easy it is to work you up when you know what you're doing, your pussy is soaked."

Her hips buck, writhing under me and I tsk, shaking my head.

"I'm going to ask you again..." I stall, "do you trust me?"

She nods enthusiastically.

"Say it kitten, I need you to say the words."

"I trust you," her voice trembles, her eyes fluttering shut as she catches her breath.

"Good," I lean across, pushing her hair away from her face and kiss both of her eyelids. Kneeling back, I reach behind me and grab a rippled glass dildo.

"No, no way," she shakes her head violently from side to side, her eyes widening as she tries to push her legs shut, but I stop her.

"You don't even know what I'm going to do yet," I run my tongue across my bottom lip then drag my teeth on it. Letting my fingers slip up and down her slick folds, I carry on teasing and rubbing her, working her back up. Pushing a finger into her, I pull to the tip and swirl her arousal round her opening, lubing her up.

"And here I was thinking we were going to need some lube." I wink at her. Her hips buck, grinding her sweet pussy on my fingers trying to take what she needs.

"Darling, I promise you, you're going to come so fucking hard... patience."

Slipping two more fingers inside of her, I stretch her while pumping in and out of her slowly.

"Crew, please, I need more, I need you."

"I know sweetheart, I know," I continue my torture before pulling my fingers out and smothering the tip of the dildo in her arousal and using it as lube.

Pressing the tip of the rounded glass tip at her opening, my fingers work her clit as I rub them in gentle circular movements.

"Don't tense princess, relax baby," I usher her, pressing the glass dildo in a little farther.

"Such a good girl, your pussy is so greedy," I groan, my cock straining against the material of my boxers. Working my fingers up faster, I rub them side to side. Her hips buck up as I push more of the glass shaft inside of her. Pulling it out gently, I let it sit at her opening as I lean over and suck her clit into my mouth and push the dildo in deeper.

"Shit," she cries out, my tongue flicking her clit and piercing.

Fucking her with the shaft of the rippled dildo, I keep the thrusts slow and deep. She pulls on the cuffs that are restraining her wrists as my tongue swirls over her sensitive bud, sucking hard. She grinds her pussy over the dildo, fucking it as I keep it still.

"Take what you need baby, take whatever you want," I pant, spreading her folds with my fingers so I can eat her like I have been dying to. She looks down, watching me fill her, knowing she has *never* been fucked like this before.

"Crew," she cries, sobbing as her legs begin to tremble but I don't stop. My thrusts into her are slow and deep but my tongue is a vicious assault on her swollen clit. "Keep doing that, please god, please."

I chuckle against her sensitive, plump flesh, "Baby, I *may* be a god, but it's not *God* doing it to you."

"I can't take it," she cries, her back arching off the bed.

"You can baby, you can take it." I reassure her, lifting my mouth off her pussy. I watch her immerse deeper into pleasure.

I push the dildo in as far as I can, my fingers finding her clit as I rub her faster. Riding her with the glass bodied shaft, her hips gyrate as I speed up my thrusts.

"That's it, oh, Crew, I can't, shit," she pants, her legs fucking shaking. I let my eyes fall to her pussy, she has her juices running down her legs, covering the length of the dildo.

"You're so wet, do you know how much of a turn on you are? How much of a *good girl* you are?" I roll my lips, licking them.

Her eyes roll in the back of her head, I edge the dildo out of her, holding it while I spend time on her clit, lowering down and sucking before nibbling on her sensitive bud.

"I, I..." she breathes, panting, her chest rising. Gliding my hand up her body, my fingers roll and tweak her nipples as I flatten my tongue and taste her. She's on the brink, her orgasm teetering and just when it's about to wreck her, I push the dildo in hard and deep, pull her clit between my teeth and pinch her hardened nipple. Her whole body convulses, and I continue working her while her body rides her orgasm, her cum running out of her pussy. I snatch the dildo away, dropping it to the bed and I feast on her, burying my tongue deep inside her as I savour every drop of her.

Chapter Thirty-Two

Cody

I STIR, THE SUN LIGHT IS SHINING THROUGH THE cracks in the wooden slat blinds. Rolling on my side, I stretch up and take a moment to let last night replay in my mind. My wrists and shoulders are sore, but in a good way. The kind of way you feel after a good work out. But mine is a post *being fucked with a dildo* way.

I nibble my lips. My nipples hardening as I think back to last night. The way his fingers played my body, tuning me the only way *he* knows. The subtle burn making itself known in my lower belly as my sex throbs. *How is it even possible to be turned on again?*

Sitting bolt upright, I realise I am alone. My brows furrow but smooth out when I see a piece of paper on the empty pillow next to me. I half smile, sliding the paper through my fingers before I begin to read.

> *Beautiful,*
> *As much as I wanted to stay spooning you this morning, I couldn't. I have reports to write up and*

work crap that I need to get done. I'll be back over tonight around five, I'm off for the next three days. Pack your bags and come and stay with me for a while, just so I know where you are, so I can keep you safe.

I'll be thinking of you today, my dildo will also be a constant reminder.

It's our time my little dove.

See you tonight.

Love, me and Dildo Darius. X

P.S. I know you're anxious, I've left a bottle of pepper spray down on the kitchen counter. Not that you need to worry, but it's there if you want it.

I smirk, rolling onto my back and take a moment. My fingers trail down my body, my sex pulsing as I slip my hand into my silk shorts. I gasp as my tips brush against my clit, my arousal still evident which only turns me on more. I let my fantasies flood my mind as I imagine Crew lowering my pussy over his mouth, savouring every part of me as he licks and sucks just how I like it. My fingers press harder, swirling my wetness through my folds as I tease at my opening then dragging my tips back over my clit. His fingers dig into my hips, moving me down and lowering me over his perfect, thick, cock and that's all it takes before I orgasm, my back arching off the bed as my body tingles from head to toe.

SCRAPING MY HAIR ON TOP OF MY HEAD IN A MESSY bun, I run my fingers through my bangs and smother my lips in lip balm. I check my phone to see the messages from the girls saying they're bringing coffee and muffins. My stomach groans. I haven't eaten since yesterday, and suddenly, I am famished. I step away and slip my slippers on when my phone beeps. Grabbing it, I smile when I see it's from Crew.

> God, I miss you. I can still taste you, still smell you, can still see you every time I close my eyes…

I smirk, nibbling my bottom lip I reply back.

> Not as much as I miss you. Well, the thoughts are mutual, so much so I had to *see* to myself this morning.

I giggle, knowing that'll rile him up. He responds.

> You little cock tease. I'm hard, at my desk. How am I going to see to that now?

I howl.

> Oh I don't know Mr Mann, suppose you'll have to wait till tonight. I'll wait for you on my knees, my mouth wide open and naked. And this time, you can use my body how you want it. Nothing is off the table.

I send it and wait, nibbling on my nail. I wait. And wait. I start to panic that I've gone a little too far when my phone pings.

I'm going to treat you like the slut I know
you are deep down, see you at 5.

My insides swarm with fire, I went to lock the phone when it buzzes again.

Naked.

I smirk, tossing my phone on my bed and heading towards the lounge.

ME AND THE GIRLS SIT ROUND THE COFFEE TABLE AND I take a sip of my oat latte.

"God, that hits the spot," I groan.

"Tired?"

My cheeks pinch. Hallie's eyes widen.

"You didn't?" Her lips play into a smile.

"Didn't what?" Mabel asks as her eyes volley between me and Hallie.

"I am assuming she got fucked last night," Tia rolls her eyes and sips her chai tai latte. "At least someone is," she mutters against her takeaway cup.

"It'll pass sweetie, bubba is still so young then you'll be back to fucking like rabbits," Mabel reassures her. I am grateful that the attention has moved from me, but as always with these rabid hyenas with a carcass, they don't drop it.

"Anyway, don't change the subject," Mabel smirks as all eyes move to me, "did you get fucked last night?"

Tia shuffles to the edge of her seat, her eyes wide. Damn. I suppose I need to give her something to get through the night feeds. I feel my smirk grow.

"Something happened, yes. But I wasn't fucked as in... you know... the way you think." My cheeks pinch with red, and I feel my insides catch alight.

"You've lost me," Mabel says, turning her head to look at Hallie and she shrugs as her eyes seek out Tia and Mabel before they move back to me. I sip my coffee, praying they drop it.

"Care to explain?" Hallie asks, sitting back in the armchair and crossing her legs.

I puff out my cheeks, breathing out the hot air that I was holding in.

"Okay, so..." I take another sip, my mouth is suddenly dry. "I told Crew I hadn't had an orgasm through sex with *he who shall not be named.*" I chime the last bit out.

"Let's just call him a twat?" Hallie turns her lips down and raises her brows as she nods.

"Twat is perfect."

"Continuing, I told him I had my bean pierced to try and stimulate my sensitivity but alas, nothing. Anyway, we had a little kiss, he spilled some words and then we ended up in the bedroom."

"Shocker," Mabel heckles and laughs.

"Fuck you," I flip her off and the girls laugh.

"Please continue, this is the most action I have seen in two years," Tia whines, stamping her feet on the floor like a toddler throwing a tantrum.

I lick my lips.

"Crew took me to the bedroom, told me to sit on the edge of the bed and disappeared. He came back with a knife..."

"Holy fucking shit, are you joking?" Hallie shrieks.

"No." I shake my head, "No I'm not. But it's not what you think..."

"It's not?" she asks.

"It's not."

"What does she think it is?" Mabel asks and looks at Tia but she shrugs.

"She thinks he was going to carve his name onto my skin, or kill me... maybe? I don't actually know."

Hallie chokes on her tea, "I didn't think either of them!"

"What did you think?" My eyes widen.

"I thought you were going to become blood buddies or something."

"Fuck's sake," I laugh, tipping my head back.

"I'm lost," Mabel interrupts.

"And me," Tia pipes up.

"Anyway, back on track... he carved his initials into my bed post, not quite sure why? Maybe to mark his territory so to speak?"

"Yeah, possible," Hallie says sipping her mocha latte.

"Then what?" Mabel shuffles in her seat.

"Then he made me strip, but I had to leave my panties on..." I sink my teeth into my full bottom lip, dragging it between my teeth.

"And then?"

"And then he cuffed me to the bed."

"And then?" Tia asks edging more towards the edge of the arm chair.

"He took my panties off with his teeth, then shredded them," I press my thighs together.

"Oh my," Tia squirms, Mabel fans her face and Hallie sits there with the best, damn poker face I have ever seen.

Silence falls over the girls for a moment. I look at my nails, hooking my knee over the other and waiting for one of them to say something.

"Continue!" Mabel shouts out making me jump.

"Jeez," I laugh, "okay, okay." Swallowing down.

"Where did I get to?" I drum my fingers on my chin.

"He destroyed your panties," Tia's voice is thick.

"Ah! Yes!" I nod, "panties," I smirk.

"Stop dragging your heels!" Mabel whines.

"Okay, okay," I hold my hand up in defence, "he cuffed me to my bed, so my hands were rendered useless. Then he finger fucked me and played with my bean and my little hoop." I smirk, wiggling my brows.

Tia crosses her legs, shuffling forward to the edge of the chair and Mabel plays with the ends of her hair.

"Sorry, but why am I feeling all horny and shit over you getting your clit played with?" Hallie exclaims.

"Cause you're a horny bitch," I pout, blowing her a kiss.

"It's not just you Hallie, I just want to go home and jump George's bones!" Mabel cries.

"Can I jump George's bones?" Tia scoops her hair off the back of her neck then lets it drop down again, she looks flustered.

We all burst out laughing before I am pressed to continue.

"Okay, so, I was loving it and then he was teasing, stretching me, yano..." I pause for a moment, "then he pulled out a glass rippled dildo, kind of looked like a baton but with curves...."

Tia chokes on her coffee. Mabel slaps her hand against her mouth. And Hallie? She just looked at me in pure disgust.

"A glass dildo?" She says as if the I've just told her I ate dog shit.

"A glass dildo." My voice is clipped, and I nod.

"What did he do with the glass dildo?" Mabel whispered.

"Why didn't he just use a vibrator or a normal, skin coloured dildo?" Tia asks but doesn't look at me.

"Because he wanted to spice things up?! Not that he needed too..." my voice heightens, I shrugged, "I have no fucking idea why he used it. I panicked, tensed up but my good god..." I stop, closing my eyes and letting the flashbacks invade me.

"So good then?" Hallie smirks.

"Fucking spectacular," I chime, my grin spreading as the girls laugh and I join them.

Chapter Thirty-Three

Cody

STANDING IN MY ROOM, I PUT MY HANDS ON MY HIPS and look at the boxes I have packed. This would last a few months, I wouldn't need to come back and to be honest, this felt like the right thing.

Pushing my bangs away from my sweaty forehead, I smile as I step towards the door. Turning, I skip down the stairs, holding onto the newel rail as I do and head towards the kitchen. I still when I see the pepper spray sitting on the work surface, padding over I pick it up and twist it round, scoffing.

"Bless him," I whisper, spinning on my heel and placing the pepper spray in my bag that's hanging by the front door. "Just in case," I say, my heart rate accelerating, skipping beats and making me catch my breath. A silly smile graces my face as I turn for the kitchen and flick the coffee machine on. Lifting my eyes, I see it's four-thirty and I am literally counting down the minutes until Crew is here. Stirring my frothy milk into my coffee, I add a sugar. Tapping the spoon on the side of my cup, I walk back into the hallway and stop dead in my tracks, my blood running ice cold when I see Julian standing in my living room.

"Julian," I breathe, panic swarming me, and I drop my coffee cup as it smashes on the floor.

"Isn't this a pleasant surprise," he smirks, twisting his fingertip into the palm of his opposite hand.

"You shouldn't be here; you were held and bail denied." I stammer, stepping back. I was trying not to tremble, but I couldn't. My hands were shaking, my whole body quivered with fear.

"That's where you're wrong. The sad thing is Cody, I never wanted to hurt you that night. I didn't *mean* to hurt you. But now, now that little prick has got involved well, now I do want to hurt you even more than I ever had in the past."

"Julian, please, you don't need to do that," I whisper, backing away but my back hits the wall. Julian closes the gap between us, a sinister smile on his face.

"Oh, but I *do*. I want to show that little cunt just how he makes me feel by taking it out on you." He scoffs, his eyes falling to my hand. "Where's your ring gone?"

"I, I..." I stammer, swallowing the thickness down, bile threatening to rise. I need to stand tall and not show him I'm afraid. My eyes move to the clock, not long and Crew will be here.

"I, I..." he mimics in a condescending tone.

"Do you know what Julian?" I snap, "Fuck you!" I spit in his face, and I wish I would have thought about my actions because his hand strikes across the same cheek as before, making my head spin.

"Stupid little slut," he grabs my cheeks, turning me to face him and squeezing tighter. "I bet you fucked him as

211

soon as I was off the scene didn't you," he grits out, his eyes wide.

I nod, smirking through his grip. He loosens his fingers so they're no longer digging into my skin. Grabbing his wrist, I pull it away from me.

"You bet I did, he made me see fucking *stars*." I know this is antagonizing him. Turning, I try to bolt but his hands are in my hair, pulling it tight and tugging me back towards him. His spare hand runs up my body and clasps my throat tightly as he pulls my back flush to his front.

"You're going to wish you never told me that," he whispers, his lips pressing to the shell of my ear. Tugging my head back hard so I'm made to look at the ceiling, my eyes prick with tears as the burn on my scalp presents itself. He knees me in the back of the legs, so I fall forward, dropping my hair as he does. He steps back, my heart is jack hammering in my chest when he takes a step back and swings his foot with force into my side making me cry out.

I tuck my legs under myself and wrap my arms round in a foetal position, but it doesn't help. He hits me with blow after blow to my body before he pounds his fist into my face. Softly and slowly his aggressive assaulting words seem to fade out, the room around me begins to spin and as much as I try, I cannot keep my eyes open. It doesn't hurt anymore. I am numb. Completely numb.

Crew will be here soon.

He won't be long.

I try to keep positive thoughts, but the longer his attack goes on, the less positive I was feeling. *This is how I am going to die.*

He is going to kill me.

Crew is going to be too late.

I'm a goner.

They were my final thoughts before everything went black.

Chapter Thirty-Four

Crew

TICK, TOCK. TICK, TOCK. TICK, TOCK.

My eyes were pinned to the clock, the last hour had dragged. I was on desk duty, and I was bored shitless. I saw the deputy walk towards me, so I sat straight in my chair and tapped the keys on my computer.

"Mann," Jack nodded at me.

"Deputy," I give him a curt nod, "how are you?"

"I'm okay, busy busy, how about you? It's good to have you back."

"It's good to be back, sir," I smile.

"Good." He lets out a shallow breath, "heard about that nutcase you bought in."

That statement piques my interest.

"Julian?" I shuffle forward in my seat as I look up at him, my brows slightly furrowed.

"Yeah."

"What about him?"

"Heard he was let out yesterday. Not enough evidence to hold him," he shrugs his shoulders up. "It's a real shame, he would have gone down for a pretty number too."

Suddenly my blood runs cold, my eyes widen.

"Fuck," I choke out, grabbing my phone and ringing Cody.

"Crew? Is everything okay?"

Ring ring. Ring ring. Ring ring.

Hi you've reached Cody...

"Shit," I slam my hand on the table and click to ring her again. Nothing.

"Crew, talk to me."

"It's Cody. I promised he wouldn't get near her, promised her he wouldn't get out," my voice was getting faster the more panicked I was getting.

"What makes you think he has gone to her?"

"Because I know. Sir, please. I need to..."

"Go, go. If I don't hear from you in twenty, I'll send a car."

And I'm gone. "Thanks!" I shout out from halfway down the hallway, pulling the door for the carpark and sprint to my car.

I floor it, metal to the floor as I rush to get to her house. My heart is beating double time, sweat is beading on my brow, my palms are sweaty as I grip onto the steering wheel.

"Come on!" I shout as I hit a red light, smacking my palm repeatedly on the wheel.

Counting down in my head until it turns green, and I speed off.

Pulling up outside her house, I pull my keys from my pocket and fiddle to find hers. Everything is a blur as I run up the stairs. I go into auto pilot and ring the doorbell. I can't think straight. I can hear the blood pumping in my ears, the noise whooshing and my heart is jackhammering against my chest, skipping beats and making me catch my breath. Shaking my head, I slip the key into the lock and twist it.

"Cody!?" I shout out as I pad down the hallway, heading towards the kitchen. Turning the corner for the lounge and that's when I see her and my fucking heart sinks to my knees, my stomach dropping when I see her black and fucking blue on the floor.

"Baby, baby," I beg, scooping her up and she whimpers. "I'm here, petal, I'm here." Delicately brushing her fringe out her eyes. He has beat her to a pulp.

Slipping my phone out my back pocket I call my deputy and tell him to find Julian and get back up here and send an ambulance.

"I've got you baby, I've got you."

Cody

Everything aches. From my head to my toes. I lay in my bed, my eyes pinned to the door as I wait for Crew to enter. I woke not long after Crew got to me apparently, I was taken into hospital and checked over and Crew was over-protective. I felt sorry for the doctors. My injuries could have been so much worse, I was in pretty good shape apart from a chipped collar bone, two broken ribs and a couple of black eyes. Julian handed himself into the police station the night of the attack. Apparently, guilt was eating him alive. He won't be given a chance of bail again and will be held until his trial.

Relief sweeps over me when Crew comes in with two cups of tea.

"How's my angel?" He asks, passing me a cup and I wince. "What hurts?"

"I'm okay, I promise," I reassure him as I take a sip and close my eyes. Nothing beats a fresh cuppa tea.

"You sure?" He looks at his watch, "you're due your painkillers, want me to get them for you?"

I shake my head, "Let me enjoy my tea first."

He climbs onto the bed and rests his back against the headboard. Silence fills the room but it's welcomed. What with the pounding headache and the constant visitors, silence is needed.

"Just in case you forgot," he trailed off watching the bedroom door, "your mum is going to burst through that door in three, two…"

"Good morning darling," mum calls as she swings the bedroom door open, "morning Crew our darling boy," she beams at him before coming to sit at the edge of the bed.

"Show me your face, let's see how those bruises are looking." She grips my chin and turns my head gently towards the window and smiles at me. "A few more days sweetie and they hopefully should start yellowing."

I smile at her, she was in such a state when she first saw me. Crew had to take her out because she went into full panic mode, which understandably she would, I'm her baby. He has been so fantastic with her and my dad and even the girls. He knows when enough is enough though, then he begins rounding them up and sending them on their way.

"I've bought everything over to cook a roast, I even made an apple and blackberry pie last night to serve with custard for dessert, how does that sound?" Her eyes are glistening, I can see she is struggling and putting on a brave face. It doesn't matter how much I reassure her that I am fine, she doesn't rest easy.

"That sounds amazing mum, really, thank you."

She slips off the bed and stands by my side as she pushes my hair from my face.

"Anything for our baby girl," My dad's voice blankets the room and I beam at him. Mum leans over and places a kiss on my forehead before heading towards the door.

"Try and get some rest," her eyes slowly move to Crew, "maybe you should come out and give her some time to nap?" My mum softly suggests to Crew but he doesn't even attempt to budge. He gives her a cocky smirk and crosses his legs in front of him over one another.

"I'm perfectly fine here, thank you," he smiles, and she rolls her eyes before closing the door.

"She loves you really," I tease, and he nudges me gently causing a small laugh to bubble out of me. Then I cry because everything hurts.

"But not as much as I love you," Crew says softly, and I turn to face him.

"Oh, I know, I love you too. You're my best friend, well, best male friend." I lick my lips and smile.

"No, Cody. I don't mean as friends." Suddenly, his face falls serious.

"You don't?" My heart is practically skipping in my chest at the words that are tumbling off his lips.

"I don't," he shakes his head, turning and placing his cup on the bedside unit and then he takes mine and places it next to his. "Cody, I fell for you from the moment I laid eyes on you, call it love at first sight if you wish but it's true. I know you feel it too, I can *feel* it. I lost you for two years because I was too fucking stubborn and scared to tell you how I felt. Coming back and knowing you were with Julian broke my heart. It made me feel sick to my stomach that he had you and I didn't. I was *envious*, no, *jealous*. Just call me

218

the green-eyed monster, because I was wearing a beautiful shade of green. I hated that he had you, hated that he got to touch you, kiss you, *love* you when all I have wanted to do from the first moment. I saw you was do everything he done. I wanted to erase all of your past, all of your firsts just so I could be them.

Your first kiss, your first boyfriend, your first *everything*. But one thing that I know for sure is, that I am never, *ever* letting you out of my sight again. I wasn't joking when I said you were mine. You will always be mine, I just need you to say it." He licks his lips, his full, wide, blue eyes volleying back and forth between mine waiting desperately for me to answer.

I swallow the lump and wipe the stray tears that have escaped.

"I'm yours," I breathe out, he chokes out a laugh then leans over to me making sure he is being gentle when tucking my hair behind my ears, his hands cupping my cheeks so softly and his lips hover over mine.

"I love you Crew," and finally, those *three words* feel so right. They're not forced or said in agreement or out of pressure. They're said because I mean them. I've meant them from the first feeling of them on my tongue. Because they were right. It's always been Crew.

I sniffle, blinking and more tears roll. His thumb pad swipes them away, as his lips edge closer to mine.

"And I love you more, my little dove."

"That's the name I like," I whisper against his lips as he kisses me.

"My little dove," he croons before dipping his tongue into my mouth and submersing me into his heavenly kiss.

I got my happily ever after, *he* is my happily ever after. I finally got the fairy-tale.

Chapter Thirty-Five

Cody

One Year Later

POTTERING ROUND THE SHOP, I STAND AND TAKE A moment. The shop is thriving, people love coming in to do some reading, buy some books and enjoy good coffee and cake and nine times out of ten they take some flowers home with them. Everything is moving along nicely, for the first time in a very long time I am so happy.

Turning, I head to the front of the shop where the florist is and the door bell chimes. I look up and beam from ear to ear when I see Luna and Taron walk in.

"Oh my god, hey!" I call out, moving through the people and hugging Luna.

"Hey, we were just walking past and wanted to see how you were getting on but by what we can see, you're getting on very *very* well." She smiles before looking up at Taron.

"Honestly, business is going great. Do you want to see the new renovation? Well, I say new, it's been about a year since it was completed."

"Yes, of course," her hand is tucked inside Taron's as she drags him behind me.

"How are you Taron? Work still going well?" I ask as we walk through the coffee shop and Luna waves at Eva who worked here when she owned it. She quickly pulls her hand out of Taron's and runs to Eva, throwing her arms round her neck they hug it out and laugh.

"Work is going really well, I am so lucky to have wonderful friends that I work with too, makes it more bearable," he chuckles, the whole time he has his eyes pinned to his wife. I mean, I don't blame him. She is beautiful.

"Yeah, I get that. I like my team here, very grateful," I push my hands into the back of my jean pocket. The bell rings and I feel him before I even see him. My skin erupts into goosebumps, my heart racing in my chest.

"Love," Crew smiles, kissing me softly on the lips.

"Hey," my cheeks pinch red. Luna bounces back over and slips her hand back inside Taron's.

"Luna, Taron, this is my husband Crew," he looks down at me and smiles, "darling, this is Luna and Taron, who I bought the shop from." I nibble my lip.

"Oh, I've heard a lot about you two," Crew laughs, reaching out and shaking Luna and Taron's hands.

"All good things I hope?" Taron smirks, his dark brown eyes glistening.

"Only good things mate," Crew pats him on the back as we begin to walk towards the renovation.

"So, how long have you been married for?" Luna asks.

"Just coming up to a year, we got engaged and Crew had some time off work. We didn't want a big fancy wedding, so we eloped to Gretna Green. Took our parents and a handful of friends and got married!" my voice is fast as excitement floods me thinking back to the memories.

"Best way to do it I suppose."

We all stop in our tracks when I get to the book nook.

"Oh wow," Luna gasps, dropping Taron's hand and walking further into the room, "oh my god, Cody. This is spectacular!"

"It's something isn't it." Proudness swarms me. Luna pulls out her phone and turns on video call, a few rings in four girls pop on the screen.

"Hey!" Luna calls out, "just a quick one."

My confused eyes bounce from Luna to Taron when our eyes catch and he smirks. "She always has to call the girls," his lips twist and I giggle.

"This is Cody, who bought the shop, say hi Cody," Luna says as she shoves her phone in my face.

"Oh god, oh, hi!" I wave awkwardly and blush.

"Girls, look at what she has done with the place," Luna chimes as she shows them around the busy room.

"Wow," they all say separately, "that looks amazing," one of the girls say.

"I know, right!?" She beams, "anyway, I'll call you back soon. Bye," she waves at her phone then cuts them off.

"You should be so proud of yourself," she steps towards me, her hands on the top of my arms, "you've smashed this."

"Thank you," I blink away the tears, "thank you for selling it to me."

She looks over her shoulder and smiles at Taron. "We both knew you were the right fit for the shop, you had the drive and the ambition to grow the shop into something beautiful," she winks, "and you done it."

I throw my arms around her, hugging her because she changed my life by letting me buy this shop.

They enjoy lunch, on the house of course, and I leave them be as me and Crew head towards the back of the shop.

"What time you finishing?" He asks as he closes the gap behind me, wrapping his arms around my waist and pulling me close. His lips brush against my vein in my neck, trailing slow and soft kisses to my ear.

"In about fifteen," I breathe, my breath hitching as he continues, "I've just had one last order come in, why?" I just about manage.

"Because I am desperate to taste you, desperate to sink my cock into your soaked little cunt. I am going to treat you like a slut, just like you like."

My cheeks burn a deep crimson red and I pull away. "Let me just sort this order, I'll meet you out front." And I scarper off before the devil comes for me himself.

Pulling the ticket from the printer, my heart drops and the ache is prominent. Rubbing my chest to try and ease the pain that is searing deep inside of me but it doesn't work. I take a moment to compose myself, swiping my cheek with my palm as I wipe away the tear that rolls from my right eye.

"Oh, Bertie," I choke, sniffling. I continued meeting up with Bertie throughout the two years that Crew was away. We still met for our coffee date every Thursday morning until a few weeks ago he stopped coming. I knew deep down that something was wrong, and his daughter confirmed it with this order. My wonderful friend Bertie had passed away peacefully in his sleep. He was finally reunited with his wife and that pain soon elevated that ache that was so deep in my chest.

I will never be able to thank Bertie for what he done and how he supported me throughout my break with Crew, he kept me going, reminding me daily that if we were meant to be we would find our way back to each other, he always held out hope we would end up back together, that we would find our way and I thank my lucky stars that it was him who turned up for my blind date and not Shane.

He only got to meet Crew a few times and the times he did, they got on like a house on fire.

I headed out back and picked the Calla Lillies and deep, red roses. Bunching them together and tying them with twine, I wrapped them, so they stayed safe until I was done. Tidying my station and shutting the shop down, I opened the door to see Crew standing there smiling, his eyes dropping to my bouquet.

"Bertie," he sighed, and I nodded. "Come on baby, let's go and see him."

Standing at the freshly filled grave, I wipe my tears and bend to lay the bouquet.

"God, I miss you," I choke on a laugh as Crew's big hands wrap around me, holding me still.

"He is always around you peach, he just dances in the wind now."

"Veto," I roll my eyes and turn to look at him.

"I love you," he smiles, pressing his forehead to mine.

"But not as much as I love you," I whisper, tilting my chin up so I can kiss him.

"Not possible, little dove, not possible..."

"Take me home."

I'M ON MY KNEES, MY EYES LOOKING UP AT HIM through my lashes as his thick cock hits the back of my throat. My eyes are streaming, I'm drooling out the side of my mouth but I don't care. All I care about is getting him off.

"Such a good girl, look at you deep throating my cock like the perfect slut you are," he groans, tightening his grip in my hair as he thrusts his hips hard and fast. My throat is burning but I swallow down just focusing on him and only him.

I'm not sure where we found the whole slut kink unlocking thing, but it happened and now it's happened, there is no going back. I let one of my hands trail the inside of his legs before cupping his balls and massaging them softly before I let my nails scratch over them ever so slightly. He tenses, his balls constricting as his cock bobs. Hollowing my cheeks, I let my lips slide down his girth and smile up at him as I keep him at the back of my throat.

"You're such an angel, look how fucking beautiful you look with your eyes streaming and your mouth so full with my cock."

I moan at his words, constantly wanting to please him when we are in the bedroom. His dominates me and I welcome it. Dragging my teeth gently along his soft, velvet like skin until the thick tip of his cock is sitting on my pursed lips. I flick the pre-cum off his tip then swallow him whole again.

"Fuck Cody," he grits, his whole body tensing, and he's lost it. His head goes back, his hips rocking forward as he fucks my mouth. Pulling him out, I flatten my tongue under his cock and let him spurt his cum down the back of my throat. Swallowing, I suck and lick him clean. He steps back, fisting himself as I lick my lips and wipe the corners of my mouth.

"You're the most perfect little slut," he grins at me while I am still sitting on my knees.

"Only for you," I smile.

He steps towards me, tucking my hair behind my ear then trailing his fingers along my jaw line until he reaches my chin. Tilting my head back to look at him like he wants me too.

"Stand up baby, I need to fuck you."

I do as he says, standing on trembling legs, I'm still feeling the effects of the earth shattering orgasm he gave me when he ate me out just before I sucked him clean.

"All fours, legs spread." His hand skims over my hips then slaps my ass cheek and I gasp.

Turning, I crawl onto the edge of the bed and stay on all fours, spreading my legs wide.

I hear the drawer go and excitement dances up and down my spine. The bed dips and I feel him behind me, his hand curling round my hip as he pulls me up, so my back is flush to his chest. His hand skims over my stomach, his finger rubs my clit before he pumps it in and out of my soaked pussy.

"I am going to fuck your ass while your dildo fucks your cunt," he smiles against my skin, his teeth grazing along my jaw as he nips.

Dropping his hands from my body, he nudges me forward and spreads my legs. He glides his finger down my ass cheeks and dips his finger inside, swirling and stretching me as he drags my arousal and spreads it over my puckered hole. I tense.

"Don't tense darling, I've had two fingers in your tight little ass and you fucking loved it so I know you're going to love my cock in there."

I whimper, my legs buckling as he finger fucks me. His fingers still inside me for a moment as he reaches for the sex toy.

"You ready baby?" He asks, pulling his fingers from me and rubbing my arousal over my ass again.

"Please Crew, please."

"All in time sweet girl," his voice is soft as he presses the tip of the thick, rubber dildo into me. Crew knows that I like being filled to the max, being stretched and filled by Crew and toys gets me off.

Pressing it a little further a moan slips past my lips.

"Your pussy is so greedy."

My hips rock back as he fucks me slow with the dildo.

"I need more," I beg, my fingers scrunching into the bedsheet beneath me.

"I know my little dove, I'm going to give you more." His voice is tight, "just warming you up," and as the words leave his lips, he pulls the dildo to the tip and holding it there as his finger slips into my tight hole. My lips form into an 'o'. Pulling his finger out to the tip, he holds and thrusts the dildo deep into my pussy making my walls clench and as he pulls the dildo out, his finger plunges in.

"I need to feel your cunt around my dick before I sink into your perfect ass."

"Crew, please."

He pulls the dildo out of me, then lines his cock at my soaked opening and pushes it in hard and fast.

"You feel so good," my pussy clenches round his cock and he groans, tugging my hair. My back arches, my neck craned as my head is pulled back until it feels like it's about to snap.

"Fuck, your pussy is like a fucking drug," he groans, gritting his teeth. "Don't you dare fucking cum."

I moan, closing my eyes as I try my hardest to hold off my orgasm. Slapping my ass cheek hard, I hear the rip of the foil packet. He pulls his dick out and after a second or two he presses the tip into my ass. He groans, his throat tight and he lets out a guttural moan. The burn is intense, and I breathe through it because I know how amazing it feels when he is finger fucking my ass, so I know it's going to feel phenomenal when his beautiful cock is fucking me there. The dildo is back being pushed at my entrance, and my body trembles. I fall forward so my upper half is on the bed while my ass is in the air. Crew lifts his leg, one of his hands on my hip while his other hand is fucking me with the dildo.

"Breathe baby," he reassures me as he pushes deeper and deeper until the resistance that I felt is gone.

"Oh fuck," I cry, as he keeps still but the dildo is slipping in and out of me.

"Rub your clit, work yourself up while I use your body and take everything from you," he slams his cock into me and I cry.

My trembling fingers find my swollen clit and I begin to rub, pushing myself closer to my orgasm while Crew is riding my ass and my pussy is being fucked with a dildo.

"Crew, I feel so..." my voice quivers.

"Full, you feel so full baby. Your ass is stretched round my cock, your body was made to take me. And your pussy," he groans, "fuck, your pussy is fucking dripping. Your arousal is dripping down your legs."

"Please, harder, I need more of you."

And he listens, his hips piston in and out of me as my orgasm builds. My walls clench as he keeps the dildo pulsing in and out, edging it, holding it at my opening and then fucking me deep with it.

"That's it, oh, oh," I cry, "I'm going to come," I moan out, my body shaking as I ride my orgasm. Crew pulls the dildo out of me then slowly slides back as he pulls out of me.

"Fucking hate those things," Crew moans while removing the condom, before he is back behind me, his cock thrusting into my pussy. "Your ass was everything and fucking more," he tells me, his cock slipping in and out of my sex, his fingers digging into my hips as he pulls me up. Spreading my legs over his thighs, I ride his cock.

Pushing myself up, I roll back down his thick cock, grinding my hips down and taking him deep his hand finds my throat, gripping tightly as my head rests on his shoulder. His hips thrust up as he meets my rocking. Squeezing my nipples, I skim one hand down my sensitive skin and rub my clit. As another orgasm teeters, the burn spreads throughout my lower belly.

"Crew," I breathe, "I'm going to come again."

"I know beautiful girl, I know," he reassures me, "I'm going to fuck you, cum inside you and when it runs out of you I am going to push it back inside you."

My legs tremble as he pushes me forward and fucks me like he's promised.

"Yes, fuck," I cry, my orgasm shattering round me as I clench around his cock, our skin slapping against each other. Crew's hand is back in my hair as he tugs it hard as he rides me hard finding his own high. Panting, he stills, falling on top of me. After a moment, he rolls me on my back and swirls his fingers inside my pussy as he pushes our cum back inside me. I smile at him when his eyes meet mine.

"What a session my little twinkle."

"Veto," I laugh, pushing him so he is on his back and I climb on top of him.

"I'm going to need a minute baby," he puffs, his hands round the back of his head.

"Oh baby, I can give you a minute, and then I am going

to enjoy you a few more times," I wink, leaning down and kissing him on the lips. "I love you," I whisper.

"I love you more, my little dove."

THE END

Acknowledgments

My readers, thank you for reading Three Words. I hope you loved Crew and Cody.

To my book bloggers, thank you for everything you do. Sharing my cover reveals, making and sharing edits and teasers for my stories, the recommendations of my books, the Reels, the TikTok videos and edits. You will never know how much your support means to me. It means the world to me. Thank you, thank you. I am forever grateful.

My BETA's, thank you for reading my first draft of Three Words, you will never know how much you helped shape this story and how much I appreciated your feedback.

Els, thank you for being there. Thank you for everything, you will never understand how much you helped me.

Robyn, my PA. Thank you for not leaving me. I love you. Please don't leave me.
     Ever.

Lea, my editor. Thank you so much for doing such a wonderful job, so grateful for you.

Leanne, once again you smashed this cover out of the park. I am so grateful that I messaged you back in 2018, and thank you for sticking with me, and for putting up with my indecisiveness.

My posies, Sophie and Harriet, thank you for join my team and doing everything you do.

Lastly, my husband. I wouldn't have started this journey if it wasn't for you.

Please give my cover model Mason a follow justcallmek9 and the wonderful Stacy Powell spcoverphotoraphy on Instagram.

If you enjoyed Three Words, please be sure to leave a review.

Love you all x

Printed in Great Britain
by Amazon

34685301R00138